THE WARWICK HEIRESS

The Warwick Heiress

Margaret Abbey

NEW ENGLISH LIBRARY
TIMES MIRROR

First published in Great Britain by Robert Hale & Co in 1970
© Margaret Abbey 1970

∗

FIRST NEL EDITION OCTOBER 1971

∗

NEL Books are published by
New English Library Limited from Barnard's Inn, Holborn, London, E.C.1.
Made and printed in Great Britain by Hunt Barnard Printing Ltd., Aylesbury, Bucks.

45000975 0

CHAPTER ONE

'I've told you, boy. I'll have no thieving beggars round my farm. Be off with you, before I set the dogs on ye.'

'But Ma'am, I only want a little food. I'm prepared to work for it, I swear. I'll do anything, for my supper.'

'I've told you, boy, I've nothing for you. My house is full of idle servants already. I haven't enough work for them to do. In these hard times one has enough mouths to feed in one's own family without strolling beggars.'

Wearily the boy leaned against the doorpost, his eyes appealing, then as the door slammed to in his face, he sighed and turned away. He pulled his ragged tunic closer about his thin body and trudged sadly back along the road. It was getting late and it was almost two days since he had eaten. He must find somewhere where he could rest for the night, under cover if possible. He looked upwards at the sky and shivered. It was heavy and overcast. Before morning there would be rain, possibly snow. Back along the footpath, he had noticed a hayrick and barn, where he might be able to rest among the hay. He gazed hastily round. It was rather near to the road. If he were caught it would mean the stocks or an irate farmer, charging him with trespass, might get him a whipping or worse, but there was no one in sight and he was far too weary to search for other shelter this night. Thankfully, he stretched out among the straw in the barn, and pulled some of it over his body for further warmth.

Piers Langham was thirteen and an orphan. The recent death of his mother had left him without a soul in the world to care about him. Piers's father had been killed at the Battle of Wakefield and he had been just four years old. With difficulty he could recall a large, jolly man, who would lift him high into the air, throw him up to the rafters and catch him. He remembered his full-throated laugh and the way his chestnut hair had waved thickly back from his forehead, the hair, that he, Piers, had inherited.

He had gone away one glad spring day, proud of his new body armour, to fight for his lord, and had not returned. Piers's mother had struggled on at the farm but, without a man to help her till the land and advise her, she had finally been turned out. A month ago she had collapsed and the kindly nuns of the convent of Our Lady at Branlingthorpe had taken them in. There she died in the bare infirmary cell of the convent. Her last words had been for him. She had begged him to go to London and seek for work as a groom or a scullion. Mother Superior had been kind and provided him with some food for the journey. He had had bad weather and worse luck. The last few days had been the worst and for two of them he had not eaten. The cold ate into his bones and he shivered as he lay among the straw.

His reverie was sharply cut off by the sound of pounding hoofs on the road outside. Piers sat up, abruptly, and listened. Whoever it could be was riding at a tremendous rate and coming this way. He stood up and hurried outside. The horseman was alone and drawing nearer to the barn. Piers stepped into the shadows, hoping he would not be observed.

As the horse drew level, he realised with a start of surprise that the rider was a girl, younger if anything, than he was. She seemed to be trying desperately to regain control of her mount. Suddenly the animal neighed with terror and rose, its fore-legs high in the air. The rider was thrown into the roadway and hit her head sharply against a stone. For one split second, Piers stood stock still, horrorstricken as the magnificent beast towered above the slight figure in the roadway, then he dashed forward and seized the rein. The girl was in direct peril of being trampled to death beneath the animal's frenzied hoofs. Piers found himself pulled into the air, felt the terrifying sensation of utter, petrifying fear and helplessness, then suddeny he managed to regain control of himself and forced the animal down, out of range of the motionless girl. With a sick feeling at the pit of his stomach, he calmed the shaking horse with gentle strokes of his hand. Gradually it quietened, until it stood still, head down, sweat running down its heaving black flanks. It was a beautiful creature and, as such, highly bred and liable to fits of nervous tension. Piers swayed a little. The suddenness of his danger had turned his knees to water.

At length, he was able to lead away the docile creature to the side of the barn and turn his attention to the still figure in the roadside. He knelt beside her and felt for her heart. He breathed a sigh of relief, she had but swooned. He bent down and gathered her into his arms. She was as light as a feather, and he, despite his thinness, was a sturdy boy. He carried her tenderly across to the barn and laid her gently among the straw.

The girl was still unconscious and Piers stared down at her a little curiously. It was evident that she was a lady of quality. Her riding habit was of blue velvet. Beneath, her dress was of some rich material trimmed with fur. He drew off her gloves and chafed the cold hands.

Rising to his feet, he went out of the barn and back along the road to a well a few yards away. There was a small wooden bucket on a chain for the convenience of travellers. He filled it with water and returned to the barn. He splashed cold water on to the still, white face. Very slowly, the dark fringe of lashes flickered and the girl opened her eyes and stared up at him. For some moments her hazel eyes held his in a blank stare, then she sat up and almost at once, her lips curved into a smile.

He watched her, amazed that she could appear so roguish after her recent terrifying experience. She braided up her shining black hair and deftly pinned it up into place, while all the time her hazel eyes appraised him from top to toe.

'How can I ever thank you? You most certainly saved my life. Never shall I forget that awful moment when Starlight's hoofs were poised over my head. I thought he would smash my skull. You are not hurt?'

Piers shook his head, but said nothing, acutely conscious of his own country dialect.

'Something must have frightened him, an animal or bird from the thicket. He is usually beautifully behaved.' She paused and regarded him gravely. 'My name is Alicia, Alicia Standish. Whom do I thank for saving my life?'

Piers remained silent.

'How grave we are and dumb too. You *can* speak?'

Piers flushed to the roots of his brown wavy hair.

'Yes, my lady,' he said awkwardly.

'What is your name?'

'Piers, Piers Langham.'

'Piers Langham.' She repeated it slowly and then gave a

7

charming little nod of her head. 'And where do you live, Piers?'

'I have no home.'

'No home?' Her eyes opened wonderingly.

'No.' He rose to his feet and turned away from her. 'We lost our farm after my father was killed at Wakefield and since my mother died, a few days ago, I am alone and homeless.'

'Oh, I'm so sorry,' her laughter-filled voice had softened and he turned back, surprised at the wealth of sympathy he detected in it.

'Thank you,' he returned gruffly and then, as though to change the subject, 'your horse is quite safe. I tethered him to a ring on the fence. He is quiet again now but his leg may be sprained.'

'I'll come at once. Oh . . . ' She made an attempt to rise, then fell back on the straw, sharply biting back a sudden cry of pain. He crossed to her side and knelt beside her on the straw.

'What is it? Are you hurt?'

'My ankle – I'm afraid I've sprained it. It must have been beneath me as I fell. Now, however am I to get home?'

'You mustn't attempt to walk on it. I will help you to mount and then I'll walk by your horse's side until you reach home.'

'But I live in the city.'

'London?'

'Yes. My mistress is behind me on the road. I should not have ridden ahead so fast.'

Piers smiled at her and tore a strip of cloth from his ragged tunic, dipped it in the water and began to tighten the improvised bandage on her ankle. She gave a sharp gasp as the icy cold water first touched her flesh and then leaned back and allowed him to complete his work without further comment.

'On which side did your father fight at Wakefield?' she asked curiously. 'My father was killed there too. That makes a bond between us.'

'I really don't know.'

'Don't know which side he was on, oh but you must.'

'I don't. My mother never did. We common folk don't bother about court bickerings.'

'Court bickerings,' her eyes flashed dangerously. 'Are you, then, not loyal to King Edward?'

8

He smiled back at her, faintly amused by her vehemence.

'Oh aye, just so long as he *is* King.'

'My father fought for the Duke of York.' She shook her head proudly. 'He died fighting bravely for the White Rose, as I might have done, had I been a boy.'

'Tilling the ground is my trade and when I can't get work I beg. I have no time to think of the Wars.'

Her voice lost its haughty note once more as she said, more gently, 'Are times so bad for you? Where are you going, Piers?'

'To London, to seek employment.'

'Have you then, some friends there?'

He shook his head. 'No one. I have no kin or friends now my mother is dead.'

She busied herself replacing her shoe and frowned a little thoughtfully.

'You will find it difficult in London without friends. When you get to London, go to the Inn of the Golden Cockerel in Chepeside. Jake Garnet, the innkeeper, was once in my father's service. Mention my name and he may be able to give you work. At the very least, he will give you food and shelter until you manage to find some. I wish I could do more, but I too rely on charity these days. Since my mother died, I am lady-in-waiting . . . ' Her voice trailed off, as she heard, as Piers too had heard, the ring of iron on stone and the sound of voices outside on the road.

Piers got up and went to the barn door and listened. The intruders might be robbers on the prowl. He would allow them to come into his sight before he disclosed the presence of the girl in the barn and one so richly clad, for he had noticed the gleam of jewels on her fingers and round her throat, when he had carried her to the barn.

Two riders came into view on the moonlit stretch of road. The woman rode well and like Alicia was richly dressed. The other rider Piers took to be a serving man, for he rode a little behind and wore a plain cloak of fustian over breastplate and jerkin. The lady halted her mount when she saw Starlight tethered to the fence.

'Alicia's mount and riderless. Oh what can have happened to the foolish child? Go and see, Walter.' Her voice was low and sweet and she was obviously well born. This Piers could tell by the proud carriage of her head and the air of authority.

9

The serving man dismounted and examined the riderless horse.

'Nothing seems to be wrong, my lady. No bruises or any traces of swellings. Perhaps she dismounted for some reason.'

'You don't suppose she has been robbed?' The lady's voice sounded agitated, as she slipped from the saddle and crossed to the man's side. Piers was quite sure, by this time, that it was safe to announce his presence. He smiled down at the girl, who nodded, and then stepped into the moonlight. Both riders swung round, startled at his approach.

'You are searching for Mistress Standish?' he enquired awkwardly.

'Yes indeed. You have seen her?'

'She is here in the barn. You need not be disturbed. She is quite safe. Her horse was startled and threw her, but I do not think she is badly hurt. She has sprained her ankle, that is all.'

'Walter, attend to the horses and you, boy, take me to her.'

Piers led her into the barn where Alicia still sat on the straw.

'Alicia, foolish girl, what made you wander off, like that? I have been so worried. You are not seriously hurt?'

Alicia shook back her dark hair and made a wry face. 'No, it's my ankle that is sprained and I can't stand. Starlight threw me, but I would have died, but for Piers.'

Piers flushed. 'It was nothing. The horse was terrified and Mistress Alicia was in some danger of being trampled beneath its hoofs. I merely held on to the bridle until he calmed down.'

'He was swung right off his feet,' Alicia interrupted. 'He risked his life for me, Anne.'

'You are a brave boy. What is your name?'

'Piers Langham, my lady.'

'Piers, I am very grateful to you. I have a fondness for the girl, in spite of all the trouble she gives us.'

As she sat on the straw beside Alicia, Piers had the opportunity to observe her more closely. She was taller than her companion and delicately beautiful. Her golden hair was just visible beneath her green velvet hood and her eyes were that unusual violet blue colour, shaded by long dark lashes. Her features were flawless and her expression gravely sweet. Here was a supremely lovely woman not in the full flower of health, however. She seemed so exquisitely but delicately fashioned, against Alicia's robust strength.

Piers went out to explain the incident to Walter, the serving man, leaving the two girls together.

Later, Walter lifted Alicia into the saddle, while Piers held the bridle rein. He felt unaccountably sad at this parting. She leaned down and whispered to him urgently.

'The Inn of the Golden Cockerel. Do not forget.'

He thanked her and awkwardly bade the little company farewell. Then Lady Anne offered her hand and he touched it with his lips. When he did the same service for the laughing-eyed Alicia, he felt her mock him, as she said, teasingly, 'Farewell, Sir Gallant. I pray you find many maids in distress, for you have yet your spurs to win.'

As they prepared to leave, the Lady Anne called Piers to her. 'Please do not take offence. I know you need money. Take this purse in token of my gratitude.'

Piers drew back as the servant handed her a small leather bag which she held out to him. 'Nay, Madam, I am not offended, but I will not accept money. I would have done as much for any creature. I thought of no danger. It happened too quickly for me to gather my wits at all.'

'But you must let me give you something.'

He hesitated. 'I would not refuse food, my lady, for to tell the truth I have not eaten for almost two days.'

Both women drew little gasps of pity and Lady Anne frowned. 'Food? I fear not. No, wait, I have a little. Walter, in your saddle bag, you have a box of pastries. Bring them to me, please.'

'But my lady, they are for your mother, sent by the Abbess, who baked them with her own hands . . .'

She interrupted him with an impatient movement of her gloved hand. 'Bring the box to me, I say, and hurry.' Muttering a little beneath his breath, the servant obeyed and handed the box into Pier's hands.

He stood and watched until a bend in the road hid them from sight and then, with a little sigh, turned and re-entered the barn. He sat among the straw and ate the rich pastries. Never had food tasted so good. He drank some of the well water and then settled himself once more to sleep. A smile curved his lips as he thought on Mistress Alicia's roguish hazel eyes. He hoped he would soon see her again in London Town. Walter's cloak had slipped open, as he handed the box of pastries to him and he had caught a fleeting glimpse of his livery

11

beneath. It was the most famous in all England, a bear and ragged staff, of course, the arms of the great Earl of Warwick. Was the sweet fair girl, who had befriended him, the younger of the Earl's daughters, Lady Anne Neville? If so, his adventure had led him into distinguished company indeed.

CHAPTER TWO

The bustling hurry in the London streets was a source of wonder to the country-bred Piers. Never had he seen so many houses and so many people clustered together. He crossed London Bridge and stared at the rows of houses and shops the dirty, barefoot street urchins, the merchants in their fine clothes picking their way through the refuse in the gutters.

Although he had not eaten since early morning, when he had snatched a new-made loaf from the open window of a farmhouse, he found himself too excited to be aware of his hunger.

In Chepeside, Piers halted before an inn displaying the sign of the Golden Cockerel. He stood irresolute before the courtyard. His clothes were dirty and torn. He looked so obviously a beggar. Would he be cursed and turned away as he so often had been?

He crossed the inn yard, and paused in the doorway. The inn was prosperous for it was crowded. He had noticed horses standing in the yard with ostlers in attendance. In one corner, a group of soldiers sat dicing. Opposite, a merchant, richly dressed, was enjoying a good supper.

'What is it you want?' Startled, Piers looked up to see a pleasant-faced, red-cheeked woman, looking curiously at him. He shuffled awkwardly. 'I mean no harm, Ma'am. I was looking for the landlord, Jake Garnet. He does live here?' There was no anger or contempt in her expression, merely curiosity. She looked him over from top to toe, hand upon her hip.

'Yes, Jake Garnet lives here. I am his daughter. What do you want with him?'

'Work, ma'am. Mistress Alicia Standish told me to come here and she said your father would perhaps find something for me to do. I'm young but I have a strong arm and I'll not shirk.'

'Lady Alicia? You know her?'

13

'I met her once and did her a slight service. She told me to come here.' She put her head on one side, as she looked at him, then she nodded briskly.

'Well, you seem honest enough and you look half starved. Come in. I'll take you to father.'

She led the way through the crowded room, to a small parlour at the back. The little room was scrubbed clean and the rushes on the floor were freshly strewn. Piers felt more awkward and dirty than ever. The girl left him and he stood quite still and waited, rather miserably, for her to return.

He looked up anxiously as the door opened and a huge, pleasant-faced man bore down on him.

'So you are the boy,' he rumbled. He took Piers's hand and squeezed it hard. 'Glad to see you. This is the boy, Bess, who saved Lady Alicia's life. Get food for him, and come nearer to the fire. The day is one of the coldest of the year and you must be starved.'

Piers sat down on a stool and held out blue hands to the welcome blaze. 'You are kind, sir.'

'Nonsense, lad. Lady Alicia told me all about you. That was a rare, brave thing you did. I love the lass, served her father, aye that I did, and saw him fall at Wakefield. I promised him then I'd serve her and I will, lad. I'll be glad to help you all I can. What think you to work in my stable as an ostler?'

'I would be grateful, sir.'

'Good, sit you here and my girl Bess will find you something hot to eat.' The older man slapped him on the back and lumbered to his feet. 'I'll have to leave you alone for a while and return to my customers. Stay here, lad, and get yourself warm.'

Piers drew his stool to the side of the large, open fireplace and luxuriated in the comforting warmth from its blaze. The firelight flickered over the pewter and brass on the dresser behind him and gave the small parlour a welcoming air. Bess bustled about the room preparing a hot meal. She set a place at the table and moved a wooden chair forward, gossiping to him brightly.

Suddenly, the jingle of harness in the doorway made both of them look up, startled. Leaning against the door-post, grim faced, stood one of the soldiers whom Piers had noticed at a table in the tap-room. A little frown creased Bess's brow, as she looked up at him.

'What can I do for you, sir? This is our private parlour.'

The soldier gave her a brief nod and, still unsmiling, he gazed past her to Piers, seated on the stool by the fire.

'I thank you, mistress, and I am sorry to intrude on your privacy. My business concerns this lad. Is your name Piers Langham?'

Piers stared back at him wonderingly. 'Yes, sir,' he said slowly, 'I am Piers Langham. What do you want with me?'

The soldier nodded. 'Come with me at once.'

A cold feeling of fear touched Piers's heart. 'Where are you going to take me, sir?'

'That I am not permitted to tell you.'

'Why?' Bess interposed, 'what has he done?'

The man swung round and frowned. 'It would be wiser, mistress, if you kept out of this affair.' Again he looked at Piers and said shortly, 'It would also be better if you came along with me willingly, young man. We want no trouble in this inn, for the sake of your friends.'

'Trouble, friend? Who speaks of trouble in The Golden Cockerel?' The innkeeper's booming tones came from the doorway and the soldier again swung round to face him.

'Oh, Father, I'm so glad you came. This officer has come to arrest Piers.'

'Arrest Piers? Whatever for, sir? Where are you to take him?'

'He will not say,' Bess nervously twisted plump hands in the folds of her apron. Jake crossed to the boy's side and looked steadily down at him.

'What is this, Piers?'

'I don't know, sir. As far as I know I have done nothing wrong – at least . . . ' Piers's voice trailed off uncertainly, as he remembered that he *had* done something against the law. He had stolen only that very morning and stealing, he well knew, was a hanging matter.

The innkeeper eyed him carefully and the sudden paleness of the boy's face was not lost on him. 'Can I have a word with him privately?' he asked.

The officer gave the innkeeper a meaning glance. 'Yes, you

may do that, but I should keep clear of this affair. It would not be good for you to cross my master.'

Jake Garnet bowed his head, and took Piers to another corner of the room.

'Now tell me honestly, lad, what trouble you are in? Keep nothing back. If I am to help you, I must know the whole truth.' Piers flushed and haltingly told the kindly innkeeper how he had stolen that morning, forced by the keenest pangs of hunger to break the law.

Jake gazed at him, keenly. 'Is that all?'

At once Piers's head was thrown back. 'Yes indeed, sir, I would not lie to you after all your kindness.' Jake continued looking at him, then nodded again briefly.

'Right. I am prepared to help you all I can.'

Piers glanced back at the officer anxiously. By this time, he had been joined by two archers, who stood watchfully at the doorway, barring the exit. Bess looked as if she were about to cry. Piers turned back to his new friend. 'I must go with him, sir, at once, or I will bring trouble upon your house. I thank you for all your kindness.'

Jake pursed his lips thoughtfully. 'Frankly, I feel it *is* the best course, lad. I will attempt to find out where they have taken you and plead your cause.' He put an arm about the boy's shoulder and led him back to the officer. Piers looked up into the stern face, while his heart beat uncomfortably fast.

'I am ready to go with you, sir,' he said, quietly and mutely held out his hands.

'If you will give me your word that you will not attempt to escape there will be no need to secure your hands,' the officer replied.

'I promise I will not.'

The officer placed a firm hand on his shoulder and they left the parlour, walked through the tap-room and out into the cold air of the yard.

'Can you ride?' The officer barked the question and Piers nodded, silently.

'Up behind me, then.' Piers sprang up and the little group of men mounted and rode out of the inn yard. No one spoke. All the men wrapped their warm cloaks closely around them for the night was extremely cold and the little cavalcade rode rapidly through the London streets.

16

Soon, the grey walls of a fortified house loomed before them and the officer called a halt. The gate was guarded but, at a word from the officer, the portcullis was lifted and the little group clattered over the cobbles and into a spacious courtyard.

CHAPTER THREE

There was a great deal of bustling activity in the courtyard. Brands, set in sconces along the wall, lighted the yard and Piers could see ostlers busy about their business. Piers was puzzled. Where had he been brought? The castle seemed the luxurious home of some great noble, not the damp prison he had expected. No one took the slightest notice of him, after he had been once told to dismount and he stood nervously still. Suddenly, the officer beckoned.

'Come, lad, this way.'

Piers followed him through the courtyard into a large kitchen, along several corridors till at last they came to a tapestry-covered doorway, and the officer who accompanied Piers spoke crisply to the pikeman who guarded it. The man stepped back and the officer ushered Piers through.

They were in a very large hall. At the far end was a raised dais, on which several richly-clad men laughed and lolled at their ease. Tapestry covered the walls and the rushes on the floor were freshly strewn. On the walls weapons were displayed and shields displaying the white rose device and on the tabards of the archers was emblazoned a white boar.

The officer walked forward, his footsteps ringing on the flagged stones, and halted before a chair set in the centre of the dais. He paused, motioned Piers to follow, and bowed low. Piers, open-mouthed with wonder at the splendour of the place, looked up at the dais. In the chair reposed a small, pale young man. He was, Piers judged, about seventeen years old. His bronze hair, which was thick and shining, hung low to his shoulders. Cold grey-blue eyes watched Piers curiously and there was a sudden silence. The young man was richly yet tastefully dressed, but even the careful cut of his elegant blue velvet houppelande could not disguise the fact that one shoulder was slightly higher than the other and the leg, care-

18

lessly flung out in repose before him, decidedly twisted.

'Richard Crookback.' To his horror Piers heard himself jerk out the words, as he realised he stood before the King's brother. It was too late however to bite them back, for the Duke had heard and the mobile lips curved in a sarcastic smile.

'Yes, I am Richard of Gloucester and, as you have observed, a partial cripple.' The voice was cold and clear and to Piers, cut like the lash of a whip. He flushed with shame at his tactlessly uttered words. There was a little silence, then the young Duke spoke again.

'Is this the boy, Walter?'

'He says he is, your Grace.'

'Speak, boy, are you Piers Langham?'

'Yes, your Grace.'

'You found him, I take it, at the Golden Cockerel?'

'I did, your Grace.'

The Duke lifted a slim white hand in a gesture of dismissal and the officer stepped back. 'Now, Piers Langham, what have you to say?'

Piers remained for a moment awkwardly silent. What had he to say?

'I stole, Your Grace, a loaf of bread from the farm, merely because I was hungry.'

'I see.' Not a muscle on the cold-featured young face moved. 'You know the penalty for theft?'

'I do, my lord, death.'

'You were hungry. That is the excuse you offer for the crime? Perhaps you were on the point of starvation.'

'That I was hungry was my reason for stealing, my lord. I do not offer it as an excuse.' Piers did not falter and his voice came clear and steady. Again there was a slight pause. When the Duke resumed speaking, there was a faint note of amusement in the voice that Piers had not noticed before.

'And did the loaf of bread taste as good to you as the rich pastries made for the good Countess of Warwick, Piers?'

Piers lifted his head and stared at the Duke, wide-eyed. Had his ears deceived him? The Duke smiled at him, one eyebrow slightly raised. 'Did it?'

'No, my lord, nothing has ever tasted so good to me in my whole life.'

'I'll warrant that's true, Dickon, the Countess has a veritably sweet tooth,' laughed one of the young men by the Duke's side.

19

'Peace, Frank, while I deal with this young thief. Tell me, Piers, have you a mind to stay in London?'

'If I live, my lord.'

'If you go around risking your life for maidens in distress you are not like to live for very long, but I have a fondness for the Lady Alicia Standish. I thank you.'

Piers flushed awkwardly and stammered out, 'It was nothing, sir. I would have done it for anyone and I have a way with horses.'

'So I should imagine. Alicia tells me you seek employment in London. What would you say to being a groom here at Baynards Castle?'

'My lord, I would indeed, but . . .'

'But? There must be no buts for those who serve Richard of Gloucester. If serve me you do, you give wholehearted loyalty to me and mine, lad.'

'I didn't mean that, my lord. I simply remembered that Jake Garnet will be anxious about me and he, too, offered me service. I would like to inform him of my good fortune.'

'Jake Garnet? Oh, yes, the innkeeper at the Golden Cockerel. He was kind to you? I'll attend to that. He shall be told and you yourself can go to the inn later in the week and visit him, but first, before you enter my service, listen to me. I wish you to choose freely. Here in the castle you will have good food and shelter, but you can get those things at the Golden Cockerel. I do not demand good work, I demand *perfect* work and will have it from all my men. You understand?'

'Yes, your Grace.'

'Then what is your answer? Choose wisely. You will find more freedom at the inn. I offer you the honour of serving the Royal House, that is all.'

Piers dropped on to his knees. 'I will serve you until I die, my lord,' he said, simply.

'Or until *I* do,' the Duke returned drily and there was a little ripple of laughter behind him.

The Duke called, and the officer who had brought Piers into his presence stepped instantly forward.

'Walter, take this lad to the stable and give him over to the care of Jan Hardy. Then send a message to the innkeeper of the Golden Cockerel explaining what has happened to the lad. Tell Jan to more suitably clothe and then feed him."

'Yes, your Grace.'

Gloucester turned to Piers. 'Serve me well and you will be happy here.'

Piers bowed low to the other noblemen and left the room with the officer. In the courtyard, the soldier paused and waited for Piers to catch up with him. 'I congratulate you, lad. I'm glad your interview with the Duke came to so successful a conclusion.'

Piers looked up at him with a slightly puzzled air. 'Do you think that the Duke knew nothing of my stealing the bread?'

'Not until you told him. How should he?'

'Well he knows now that I am dishonest,' said Piers with a rueful grin.

'Does he?' The older man shrugged and then said, quietly, 'Serve him well. He is a good master, though somewhat stern.'

'You have known him for a long time?' Piers enquired.

'I served the House of York before he and his brothers were born. Of all the Duke's sons, I would lay down my life for young Duke Richard,' the soldier said simply, then more quickly, 'here comes Jan Hardy now.'

Piers looked up and saw coming towards them the ugliest man he had ever seen. He was short and squat, his bandy legs proclaiming one who lived among horses. His hair was thin and greying, his features rugged with a huge nose and large, heavy mouth. Yet, in spite of all this ugliness, Piers thought he had never seen a man with a more attractive smile.

'Good evening, Jan. What a night,' the officer greeted him with a smile.

'Aye, it couldn't be worse, Walter, if it snowed, but who is this?'

'The Duke orders you to take charge of this lad, Jan, and lick him into shape as one of your grooms. He did the Duke a service and he has some knowledge of horses, but first, you are asked to feed and clothe him.'

The short man grinned down at Piers and thoughtfully rubbed his chin. 'By the look of him, Walter, he needs clothes, food and a rest. Come with me, lad, and we'll search for food first. I'll warrant it's your most pressing need.'

Piers bade farewell to the officer and obediently followed his new superior. Jan led him into the kitchens, where he shouted for a scullion. At once there was a hurry to obey his orders, and in ten minutes Piers was seated before a steaming bowl of stew and a platter of new bread. Gratefully he ate, while Jan sipped at a tankard of ale opposite and questioned him about home and parentage.

'Well, lad,' he said at last, 'you'll be happy enough here if your work satisfies me. Now, come with me and I'll find you a place to sleep.'

He took Piers into a large, bare room in the servants' quarters. Down each side were low truckle beds, each equipped with straw mattress and woollen blankets. Piers was assigned one in a corner and given a large, wooden chest to stand beside it, in which he might keep any possessions he was likely to acquire. Jan left him, after giving him instructions as to where to find him the following morning and at what hour.

That night, warm and comfortable beneath his woollen blanket, he blushed with shame, as he thought of his foolish words to the Duke. 'Richard Crookback, indeed!' he must guard his foolish tongue if he were to serve in court circles most certainly.

CHAPTER FOUR

Piers whistled happily as he set about his morning task of polishing the harness. It was late spring and the sun shone warm on his bared forearm, giving promise of a fine warm day. Jan looked up as he walked across the court and, nodding briefly, disappeared into the stable.

Piers had altered during his months of service in the Royal House. He had grown taller and plenty of good food, warm clothing and rest had changed the thin pinched-looking boy into a sturdy, well-proportioned youth. He enjoyed his work and Jan Hardy was more than satisfied with him. He was friendly and honest and soon made friends among the stable hands.

One enemy Piers had made in the household, Charles Beaumont, a squire in the household of the Duke of Clarence. Beaumont was a handsome, haughty-featured young nobleman with golden hair and curious light blue eyes. Piers, unfortunately, had failed to hold his horse steady one day as the young squire prepared to dismount. The horse reared and the young man was thrown into the mud to the considerable amusement of a group of his companions who happened to be in the courtyard. Crimson with anger, Beaumont rose to his feet and struck at Piers savagely with his riding whip.

'Clumsy fool,' he screamed, 'can you not do your work better than that?'

Piers stepped back, pale with mortification, a red weal marking his right cheek. He attempted to stammer out an apology, but only succeeded in feeling more awkward and foolish than ever. Suddenly a cold, hard voice broke across the babble of the yard and everyone was still.

'Piers – Piers Langham, come to me.' The Duke of Gloucester had ridden into the yard and was sitting surveying the

23

scene. Slowly, Piers crossed to his side and stood, head down, waiting.

'Look at me.' He lifted his head and looked obediently into the cold grey eyes. The Duke lifted one hand and turned Piers's cheek to the light.

'You did this, Charles?' he enquired, coldly.

'Yes, your Grace,' Charles Beaumont flung back his head proudly, though his voice betrayed his uneasiness.

'It is not part of your duties to chastise the grooms. No doubt you have some good reason, which I am sure you will render to your master and myself. Kindly await me in the Great Hall.'

The boy turned and flung off, out of the courtyard, still furious with rage. The Duke released Piers's chin abruptly. 'And you, Piers, go and have your hurt attended to,' he said briefly.

Just what occurred in the Great Hall Piers never knew, but evidently the young squire had been severely reprimanded for he never forgave Piers and took every opportunity to slight him and find fault with his work.

Jan Hardy came out of the stable, holding a section of harness in his hand.

'Piers,' he said. 'I want you to take this to William Sansom, the saddler on London Bridge, and ask him to stitch it. Leave it with him and I'll collect it tomorrow. Leave that. I'll get one of the others to finish for you. Get cleaned up and then you can be off at once.'

'Jan, may I go to the Golden Cockerel?' Piers asked eagerly.

'Yes, you may do that, when you've completed your errand. Don't be late as the portcullis will be lowered at dusk and it will not be so easy to be admitted to the castle.'

Piers rode into the city, for Jan knew he could be trusted with one of the horses. His errand was soon completed and he spent the rest of the afternoon at the Golden Cockerel. It was getting dusk when he took leave of his friends, mounted and prepared to return to Baynards Castle.

He noticed that most women and the unarmed and the elderly were hurrying home. The less salubrious of the London streets were haunts for footpads and numerous armed bands of robbers. Piers was glad that he was mounted and fingered the small dagger at his belt, a present from Jan for some slight service. It was one of his most treasured possessions.

He was almost out of the city when he heard the sound that made him pull up his horse sharply and sit still, listening intently. It was faint and muffled, but there was no doubt in his mind that it had been a cry that he had heard. Yes, there it was again and accompanied by a shuffling, slithering sound as if a fight was in progress. Piers hesitated for only a fraction of a second, then, judging the direction of the sound, he galloped towards it down a dark, noisome alley. Some yards away from him, two figures struggled, a thick-set heavy figure of a man and a slighter, slim form. The light of one of the torches fell on the girl's torn cloak of rich red velvet. Piers stayed only an instant to weigh up the situation, then hurled himself out of the saddle and on to her assailant. Taken by surprise, the man let go and Piers heard her panting breath as she tore herself free and then the sound of her running feet on the cobblestones. Furious, his opponent lunged out with a powerful fist. Piers was hurled to the ground with such force that the breath was knocked from his body. His head struck the ground and he experienced sudden excruciation pain at the base of his skull. Slowly, he raised himself to a crouching position and shook his head to try to clear the red mist which had formed before his eyes.

The thief stood a few feet away from him, his breast heaving rhythmically with the recent exertion. Piers saw with a sudden pang of fear that he had drawn his dagger and stood, one hand on hip, waiting. At the end of the alley, Piers saw the girl he had rescued. She stood watching, without moving, one hand placed on her heart. It seemed an eternity while the two combatants stared at one another and Piers knew suddenly, quite clearly, that for the first time in his young life he was to be involved in a fight to the death. His opponent had every intention of killing him. He gave himself only time enough to get his breath, then he rose to his feet and the two closed with each other.

Warily they circled, each with his dagger ready to pierce the other's guard. The footpad leaped at Piers and the torchlight flickered wickedly on his blade. Piers dodged and parried the thrust, then swung up his own arm in a swift, stabbing movement. The thief sprang back with a sudden animal cry of pain. Piers grunted with pleasure. First blood to him. Then again he was attacked. The other man was heavier and bull-like in his strength. He made powerful lunges, which Piers, who was lithe and slight, was able to avoid. Then abruptly he changed his tactics and flinging out a powerful hand, seized Piers's throat in a merciless grip. Momentarily off his guard, the boy was borne backwards and fought to free himself from the stranglehold of his assailant. This seemed impossible. Tighter and tighter the man squeezed and Piers began to lose his senses. A red mist swam before his eyes and his dagger hung limply in his hand. He struggled weakly and heard the man's heavy breathing, as he forced the boy's head back and back, until it seemed that his neck must break. Then, dimly, he heard the quick patter of feet on the cobbles and a startled shout. Miraculously, the merciless grip on his throat relaxed and he was flung to the ground once more.

A sense of urgency forced him to his feet, in spite of an over-whelming desire to let his body's weakness have its way and lapse into complete unconsciousness. He sprang up and searched for the dagger, which had fallen from his nerveless fingers. Then he realised what had occurred. The girl, clearly under-standing his danger, had hurled herself upon his opponent's legs and borne him to the ground. Piers sprang once more to the attack and in a matter of seconds it was all over. The thief had been forced back against the wall of a house, with Piers's dagger at his throat. The man stared at him dully.

'All right, young master, finish it.'

'No,' the girl's voice arrested him. 'Let him go.'

Piers stared at the man, noting his tattered tunic and pinched, vicious face. He remembered the occasion on which, he himself, had stolen out of necessity to keep himself alive, and he nodded briefly. Stooping, he picked up the other's dagger.

'You heard. The lady is merciful. Go.'

The man stared at him and then as Piers lowered his dagger point, he flung a mesh purse in the girl's direction and slouched off. Once out of the courtyard, they heard him break into a run.

Piers rubbed his bruised throat and sheathed his dagger.

'For a moment I thought my last hour had come. Thank you kindly, mistress. You showed great presence of mind. Had you not tackled him, he would have strangled me.'

The girl made no answer and the light of the torches flickered over her slight, girlish form and touched on her long dark hair, freed from its confining hood by the struggle through

26

which she had just passed. Piers heard a soft laugh in the half-darkness.

'Piers Langham – Piers Langham, what would I do without you? I swear you follow me around to help me in distress.'

'Alicia, Mistress Standish,' Piers launched himself forward with a glad cry, then said more anxiously, 'you are not hurt?'

'No. Thanks once more to you,' Sir Gallant,' she replied laughingly, holding out her hands to him, 'and you, Piers, are you injured?'

He gave a rueful laugh. 'Well, I think I'm all in one piece, though, truth to say, he had a punch like an ox. My jaw aches now.' He rubbed it tenderly, then gave her a slightly crooked grin, 'and my throat will be bruised for a month. By the Cross, I thought I was a dead man. Thank you, my lady, for saving me.'

She turned from him and he heard a swift, rending sound, then she came over with a piece of white linen, torn from her shift.

'Come, there is a water trough over here, let me bathe your face.'

He limped a few yards to where a rectangular trough had been erected for the purpose of watering horses. He sank down at its edge, while Alicia busied herself, dipping the linen into the water and bathed his bruised throat and jaw. She then cleaned up an oozing wound on his forehead, where he had evidently been caught by his opponent's dagger during the struggle.

'Mistress Standish,' he said at last, 'whatever were you doing here, in the city, alone and unguarded?'

'I visited an old friend of my mother's, and it was late when I left. She lives alone, being too poor to keep a serving man, so I had to return alone for there was no one to escort me.'

'If you will allow me, ma'am, I will escort you the rest of the way,' Piers said quietly.

'Gladly, Piers, for in truth I am afraid to go alone, but what of your duties?'

'I have none till the morning. Come, mount my horse and I'll walk beside you.'

He assisted her to mount and they continued their journey. Alicia soon recovered from the effects of the attack and once again Piers marvelled at her ability to shake off fear and pain so swiftly.

'Tell me, Piers, are you happy in your work?' she asked, thoughtfully.

'Very happy I can never thank you enough for what you did,' he returned fervently.

'It was little enough. Gloucester was visiting the Earl and we told him about the affair. He was impressed and offered to take you into his service. I knew you would want for nothing in such a position, so I begged him to do that, and told him where you might be found.'

'So that was how it was,' he laughed and proceeded to tell her of his assumed arrest, his confession to the Duke and then, of his recent enmity with Charles Beaumont. She frowned at this point in his narrative.

'Be careful, Piers. He comes from a powerful family.'

'I will, never fear.'

'Tell me,' she said, gazing at him earnestly, 'what do you think of the Duke?'

'Gloucester, you mean? I both admire and pity him. Admire him for his courage and pity him for his terrible infirmity, which must be intensely irksome.'

'But do you like him?' she urged.

He looked at her thoughtfully and rubbed his chin, an action unconsciously copied from Jan Hardy. 'Like him? Well, that's hard to say. He has little of his brother's charm but he is a good master to those who serve him well.'

She nodded, as though satisfied and the conversation drifted into other channels until at last they reached the Earl of War-wick's town house.

CHAPTER FIVE

Alicia dismounted in the shadow of some shrubs. 'Most of the womenfolk will have retired for the night,' she whispered to Piers. 'If I can slip in unnoticed, it will save lengthy explanations. Goodbye, Piers, my brave one. Once more I must thank you for coming so swiftly to my aid.'

Piers kissed the tips of her fingers, humbly. 'You know where to find me, if ever you should need me, Mistress Standish.'

Her voice softened, as she replied, gravely, 'Indeed I do. Now goodbye. We shall meet again.'

Then she was off, running like a deer across the grass and into the shrubbery, her dress held high, so that she might not trip over its long train. She turned back just once, and he heard her whisper, urgently, 'My room is the fourth one from the left side of the house. I will place a light in the window,' then she disappeared into the darkness.

Piers waited for a few moments, then led his horse into a thicket on the opposite side of the road and, on foot, skirted the building, arriving at length at the back of the house. There he stood still for some time, silent and watchful. Then he saw it. In the fourth window a candle, passed swiftly to and fro across the pane. Alicia's signal, she was safe and presumably had not been missed. He rose from his cramped position on the grass. Then he stiffened. At the opposite corner of the building he could see a tower-like structure and beyond it a second-storey window equipped with a small iron balcony. A girl stepped on to it and light behind her touched her soft fair hair, so that it gleamed like burnished gold. It was Ann Neville.

She leaned forward over the balcony rail and spoke softly to someone beneath. Naturally curious as to the identity of the gallant who spoke secretly to Warwick's daughter at this hour, Piers crept silently through the shrubbery, so as to be nearer to the guilty pair. Once or twice a twig snapped under his feet and he waited in agony, thinking he must be discovered but no one took the least notice and at last he was able to creep into a group of bushes immediately behind the tower and command a good view of the balcony and whoever stood beneath.

A hurriedly suppressed exclamation left his lips as, peering stealthily from his hiding place, he saw Anne Neville's visitor clearly for the first time. The moon came from behind a cloud at that moment, and there was no mistaking that familiar slight figure. Its pallid beams touched fleetingly the bronze hair and presented a clear silhouette, one shoulder higher than the other. Richard of Gloucester stood beneath the window to talk with Warwick's younger daughter. Piers decided to leave and at once. It would be fatal if the Duke found him here, watching. He rose, then saw Ann Neville drop something down from the window, which the Duke stooped awkwardly to pick up. It was a single white rose.

What occurred immediately afterwards was to remain in Piers's memory as a confused blur. As the Duke bent down, presenting his back to the shadowy bushes behind, Piers saw the moonlight flash wickedly on a steel blade above him. Horrified, he shouted a warning.

'My Lord of Gloucester, look behind you!' At the same moment he dashed forward. There was a muffled cry, a sound of slithering feet, interspersed with heavy panting breaths, then a shuddering moan. Piers dashed up in time to see the Duke rise to his feet, grim-faced, and deliberately clean his dagger on a white kerchief. Beside him on the grass lay the unknown assailant. Piers knelt down by the still form. He saw at once that he was dead.

'Well, whoever you are, boy, I suppose it was you I thank for uttering so timely a warning,' said that clear, cold voice Piers knew so well.

'Aye, my lord,' Piers said quietly. 'Are you safe?'

'Safe enough, though I'm losing blood fast from a wound in my left arm, fortunately not my sword arm. At your cry I turned and received the blow in my arm. Without warning, it would have been buried in my back.' He indicated the prostrate form at his feet. 'Is he dead?'

'Yes, your Grace. You are hurt, sir. May I help you?'

The Duke lurched a little against him and nodded briefly. Piers led him over to a fallen log.

'If you will sit here, sir, I will try to stop the bleeding with your kerchief.'

The Duke turned and looked back just once at the house. The light in the tower window had been extinguished, but Piers knew that Anne Neville still stood there in an agony of suspense, waiting in the darkness. The Duke lifted his uninjured arm in salute, then he allowed the young groom to help him to the log. He sank down heavily and Piers began swiftly to rip away the rich material of his doublet sleeve to lay bare the wound. As he did so, he felt his arm suddenly seized in a merciless grip and a cold voice said, sharply, 'Piers Langham? What are you doing here in Warwick's garden? Did you follow to spy on me?' The sudden venom in the Duke's tone startled Piers and he slipped to the ground, as the iron grip on his arm was just as suddenly released.

'No indeed, my Lord. I am here quite by accident.'

'I think you had better explain this accident,' the Duke said grimly.

As quickly as he could, Piers explained how he had been sent into the city by Jan Hardy, his subsequent rescue of Alicia and finally how he had brought her home, he ventured to look up into the stern face above him, he saw that the black scowl had relaxed and the young Duke was shaking with silent laughter.

'Oh Piers, how many more maidens in distress will you find to aid, or is it to be Mistress Alicia alone who will be favoured by your attentions? Nay, lad, don't look so crestfallen. I'm not angry. How could I be? This time it is I too who am in your debt. I regret my hasty words, but we of the Royal House make it a habit to trust no one, not even those who term themselves our friends.'

Relieved, Piers once more turned his attention to his task. It was merely a flesh wound which would soon heal, but it was bleeding profusely. He took the Duke's white kerchief, tore it into strips, and tightly bound up the gash.

'I see you number surgery among your many accomplishments,' the Duke said as the boy completed his work. 'Help me up Piers. This leg of mine is stiff.'

Faintly surprised at this command, Piers obediently hastened to assist the Duke to his feet and he nodded in the direction of the roadway.

'You will find my horse over there.' He leaned heavily on

Piers's arm as they crossed the road, where they found the Duke's stallion tethered to a post. The Duke mounted and turned to look down at the young groom.

'Best mount behind me, lad.'

'I have a horse of my own, sir.' Piers indicated it with a motion of his hand.

'Then ride with me.'

When they arrived at Baynards Castle the portcullis had been lowered for the night. At Gloucester's imperious command, it was at once raised and the two rode into the courtyard. Jan Hardy came to take the Duke's horse and he raised his eyebrows in surprise at the sight of Piers. The Duke dismounted and nodded to his head groom.

'Take both horses, Jan. Piers, accompany me, please, I may need you.'

Piers followed Duke Richard into the castle. He had never before been inside the Duke's private apartments and he marvelled at the elegant simplicity of the furnishings and hangings.

Richard flung himself down on a settle and smiled up at Piers, who hovered hesitantly in the doorway.

'Do you think you could find me some mulled wine and bring water to cleanse this wound of mine?'

'At once, Your Grace.' When Piers returned with what was required, he found that the Duke had divested himself of his doublet and had removed the blood-soaked emergency bandage.

'I'll get my surgeon to examine this tomorrow,' he said. 'For the present, it will suffice if we keep it clean. Put the wine down, lad, and come over here.'

Piers obeyed him and helped him to bathe and put on a fresh bandage, then assisted him into a furred robe and removed his long riding boots. Richard sipped his wine thoughtfully and watched the boy about his unfamiliar tasks.

'I wonder,' he said at length. 'A squire learns how to do many things, among them when to speak the truth and . . . when not to speak at all.'

Piers flushed hotly.

'You can trust me to be discreet, my lord.'

'It is well.' There was a slight silence then the boy asked, 'what do you think will happen to the body?'

'Doubtless it will be discovered and identified.'

'There will be questions asked.'

'True.'

Again there was a pause and Piers busied himself in collecting together the articles he had used to attend the Duke's wound.

'You have enjoyed your work in this house?'

'Very much, your Grace.'

'Good. Jan is satisfied with your work. He tells me you are most conscientious.'

'He is very kind to me.'

'But Charles Beaumont is not.'

Piers looked up startled and the other smiled. 'I notice more than you think I do. You made an enemy I'm afraid. Watch him. He comes from a powerful family. Help me to my room. This leg of mine is over weary tonight.'

Once again, that feeling of everwhelming pity filled Piers's heart, as he watched the Prince rise, then leaning heavily upon Piers's arm, limped into the inner room.

'Does your leg pain you, my lord?' he asked quietly and then, shamefaced, stammered out an apology. Full well he knew the Duke hated any reference to his infirmity. The Duke gave that cool little laugh with which everyone in the household was familiar.

'It aches . . . from hip to the toe, but otherwise I cannot complain. Thank you, you can go now. I think you will make an admirable squire when once you have overcome your nervousness.'

Piers smiled and moved to the door. 'I was born to farm work, my lord, to tend horses, not nobles.'

'One must be ready for anything in this life, Piers.'

'My mother said that, sir.'

'She was wise.'

'Do you require anything further, my lord?'

'Not tonight, thank you. Good night, my trusty squire.'

CHAPTER SIX

Piers was up very early the following morning. There was a great deal of work to be done before breakfast. At ten o'clock Jan nodded to the group of stablehands and, thus dismissed for a break, they hurried out into the sunlight. Piers was relating some of the town gossip he had heard and so busy with his tale was he that he failed to notice the sudden hush which had fallen on the group until a cold voice broke into his narrative.

'May I ask who gave you permission to absent yourself from your duties to waste time in idle chatter with the stablehands?'

Piers looked up startled. Richard of Gloucester stood leaning on an ebony cane, his grey eyes surveying the lounging group. 'Well, Piers Langham,' he said impatiently, 'I'm waiting for an answer.'

'Why, my lord, I . . . ' Piers broke off, uncertain what to say. 'Jan Hardy gives us permission to have a short break in the middle of the morning.'

'I am not concerned, Piers, with what the grooms do. That is entirely up to Jan Hardy. What I am concerned about is what *you* do. I have not yet seen you this morning. How do you imagine I dressed without your aid?'

'But, my lord . . . '

'Again, I repeat, who gave you permission to absent yourself from your duties?'

'Why, your Grace, I've been working all morning. There were horses to groom and harness to polish . . . '

'The duties of my squire are to attend me and to come to me only for orders.'

'Your squire, my lord?'

'Did I not say, last night, that you would perhaps make a good squire when you overcame your awkwardness?'

34

'But I thought your lordship was joking. It never entered my head to suppose that you really wished me to attend you.'

'When you know me better, Piers, you will understand that I never waste time in idle jokes. Present yourself in my apartment in ten minutes' time.'

With this, he limped off into the castle. Piers stood, staring after him. The other grooms moved a little from him, as though already he had become someone apart from them.

Piers presented himself as he had been bidden, at the door of the Duke's room. He was seated at the desk, busy with some documents, but he looked up at the boy's approach and motioned to him to enter.

'I am truly sorry if I have displeased you, my lord,' Piers stammered. 'I understood you merely asked me to help you yesterday because you did not wish others to know what had occurred. I didn't realise the position was to be permanent. Such an honour never entered my head.'

The stern lips relaxed in a smile. 'I realised that in the courtyard. Perhaps I was teasing you a little.' He sat regarding Piers very carefully, as though he would read his every thought. 'I need a personal attendant, but I must and will have someone whom I can trust.' He paused and Piers looked up at him earnestly.

'I have been watching you. You are brave and resourceful and I believe, discreet. I am minded to try you out, but first you must understand that your duties will be heavy. You will attend me at meals, help me to dress, clean and look after my armour. If I ride to war, you will accompany me and my horse will then be in your charge also. I will not suffer a fool or a laggard in my service. I am a royal prince and as such must perform tasks no other knight need do. Sir Francis Lovell is prepared to take you into his household. There you may serve him in any capacity he thinks fit. He will deal well with you for my sake. Think hard, Piers – Sir Francis would be a kind master.'

'I wish to serve Richard of Gloucester.'

The Duke looked at him intently and Piers looked fearlessly back at him. No words were said. The Duke turned away and nodded briefly, then he rose and led the way to a courtyard at the rear of the castle.

They passed out into the sunlight and headed for a group

of richly dressed young noblemen talking and laughing on the grass.

'Jehan, I wish to speak with you.'

From the group a man detached himself, came forward and bowed to the Duke. He was about fifty years old, dark, stockily built, every inch a soldier.

'I have a new pupil for you.' Gloucester looked round and his gaze fell full upon Charles Beaumont's haughty young features. 'This is Piers Langham,' he said, steadily holding that young man's gaze with his own. 'He is my personal esquire and will join you at your studies. I trust you will help him in every way possible.'

There was a faint murmur of assent. Piers flushed and the Duke smiled down at him. 'Jehan will teach you how to bear arms, listen to him well. In the future your life may depend upon what you learn now. These are your new companions. Stay with them until midday. That will be all, gentlemen.'

Each man in the group bowed gracefully. Piers flushed with shame as he noticed Charles Beaumont's glance of scorn, presumably levelled at his own awkwardness.

When the Duke had gone, Jehan Treves looked down at Piers. 'Can you ride?' he asked.

'Yes, sir.'

'Good, then get a mount from Jan Hardy. We are going for a canter.'

The ride was a pleasant one despite the fact that his seat on the horse was criticised the moment he joined the group. 'Sit up, lad, you're not a farm hand,' Jehan snapped at him.

As they cantered through the city, the most elegant of the group drew rein and waited for Piers to catch up with him. 'Don't mind Jehan's bark,' he said lightly. 'It's his job to lick us into shape.'

Piers threw the youth a look of profound gratitude. He was small boned and dark, his expression unusually indolent.

'I'm Guy Tremaine,' he said quietly. 'I serve Sir Francis Lovell.' The boy glanced at him casually, but Piers knew that in that one brief examination he took in his rough garments, workman's hands and air of clumsiness. They rode on together in companionable silence and at length returned to the castle. No longer now was Piers to eat in the kitchen, but he must wait on his master at table and then eat with the other squires in the Great Hall. He watched as Guy served Sir Francis

Lovell with wine, standing behind him respectfully and at the close of the meal, holding out a finger bowl for his master and Duke Richard.

At the end of the day he assisted his master to undress. The wound made it difficult for the Duke to divest himself of his doublet and Piers suspected it pained him, though he made no complaint.

During the days that followed, Piers learned much. In Guy Tremaine he found an ally. The slim youth with the bored air proved a lively companion and the two became firm friends. Guy encouraged him and gave him much useful advice.

One afternoon the Duke sent for him, 'Come in, Piers. There is someone here I wish you to meet.' In the room was a tall pale young man dressed in a monk's habit. 'This is Brother Martin. I wish you to learn to read and write, Piers. You may have to handle my dispatches. Brother Martin will teach you and I know you will work hard and learn all you can.'

Piers proved a sorry pupil. Although Brother Martin was exceedingly patient with him, the boy's slowness must have exasperated him. To Piers, the long hours spent in painstakingly copying his letters and spelling out his sounds were sheer torture. But, in spite of his constant grumbles, it was with a sense of pride that he first inscribed his name in crooked, uneven letters.

To Jehan Treves he proved a more promising pupil. His skill with the lance, dagger and broad sword grew gradually each day. He loved the hours spent in the tilt yard and finally only Charles Beaumont could be deemed his superior in the use of arms.

One hot afternoon, Jehan assembled his group of pupils in the tilt yard, to practise their skill with the quintain. Perhaps it was the heat, or perhaps an unusual clumsiness, proved the undoing of each of them. Jehan stood with a black scowl on his face, as each youth rode at the quintain, lance held steadily and found himself as swiftly grovelling in the dust.

'One last challenge, Stable Knight,' Charles Beaumont called jeeringly, as he skilfully kept his seat on his pure-bred mount. 'I'll warrant you'll bite the dust.'

'Before you begin to boast, Sir Gallant, let us be sure *you* can do it,' snapped Jehan irritably. Charles swung round with a light laugh.

'I'm prepared to bet on it. What will you lay against my

37

jewelled sword belt, Stable Knight, that I succeed and you fail?'

Angry colour mounted to Piers's forehead. 'Stable Knight' was the epithet Charles had bestowed on him, in remembrance of his days of service as a groom. Not for a moment did the young noble allow him to forget his humble descent.

'I have very little to wager with, but I'm prepared to accept the challenge.'

'What about the dagger you wear?' Piers glanced down at Jan's present to him.

'Very well, then.'

'Will you ride first?'

'No,' Piers looked back at him evenly. 'I will always allow you to take the precedence your birth entitles you to.'

Charles gave a scornful laugh, then suddenly he raised a hand in salute. Above them on the balcony, the Duke of Clarence had stepped out with the Duke of Gloucester beside him. Between them now stepped another figure, a giant of a man with red gold hair and grey eyes, the King himself. His voice rang out over the stilled courtyard.

'How goes it with your pupils this hot day, Jehan?'

Charles Beaumont's haughty young voice rang out in answer. 'We have fixed a wager, your Grace. I have challenged Piers Langham here to prove that his skill with the quintain is greater than mine, my jewelled belt against his dagger.'

'Well said.' The King laughed, his hand on each of his brothers' shoulders. 'What say you, George and Dickon?'

'It likes me well,' Clarence nodded. 'Do well, Charles and I'll double your reward. I'll give you the cloak you took such a fancy to.'

'It is mine, sir.'

'Have I your permission, my lord, to ride for you?' Piers asked, looking up at the slight, still figure of his own master.

'Of course.'

Piers squared his shoulders. He was not riding now for his own glory. He rode for Richard of Gloucester. Before him on its cross beam, the heavy weighted quintain hung. One false movement would bring its weight crashing down on his shoulders as he rode beneath, bearing him to the ground. Jehan was speaking to them. His own horse pawed the ground, impatiently.

'Take the best of two attempts. Be cautious now. Judge carefully.'

With the briefest nod of his head, confident of his success, Charles rode to the end of the yard. His horse's hoofs thundered forward. His lance caught the shield full in the centre. It swung back and he rode gracefully through. There was hearty applause from the small group of spectators. With a beating heart, Piers rode forward. He clutched his lance tightly and lunged with all his might at the shield. It swung back and he ducked as he rode beneath, just too late. The bag struck him heavily and only with the utmost difficulty did he keep his seat.

Charles bowed mockingly as he prepared to make his second attempt. Piers was furious with himself. Slight as the breeze was, he had forgotten to judge it correctly. He must do better this time. He heard, for the second time, the thunder of Beaumont's horse's hoofs over the cobbles, then the 'whack' against the quintain. He ducked, rode beneath – too late. He, too, in his triumph had forgotten to judge the direction of the wind. To his utter chagrin, he found himself struck with overwhelming force, and landed sprawling in the dust.

Gloucester glanced down at Piers. He said nothing. Piers knew his meaning. If he too failed in this attempt, Beaumont would be judged the victor, for the bag had struck him in the first trial, although it had failed to unseat him.

He weighed the lance in his hand and looked up at the swaying quintain. Then, gently, he urged his mount forward. He felt the wind fan his cheek and lunged swiftly. The quintain swung back. He whispered urgently to his horse, felt the bag high in the air above him, then he was through. Turning, he saw it swing back, too late to touch him.

'Well done.' The King's shout rang in his ears and, flushed with his exertion, he drew rein before the balcony, his eyes seeking those of the Duke. 'Here, lad,' the King was bending down to him, 'A mark of my approbation.' Piers stared wonderingly at the emerald ring, flashing green fire in the sunlight, in the King's hand. Gloucester nodded slightly and Piers bowed in the saddle, then reaching up, accepted the costly gift and slipped it on his finger. The King smiled genially. 'A pupil to be proud of, Jehan.'

'Indeed, sire, he works well.'

'Well done, Piers,' the Duke said quietly. Piers flushed with

39

pleasure. This was all the praise he desired.

'They both ride well. You have a good squire, George, too,' the King said jovially. 'Nay, lad,' this to Charles, 'don't be crestfallen. It can happen to the most skilful of us. I wouldn't like to recall how many times it happened to me.' Then, with a smiling nod, he left the balcony, followed by his brothers.

Later that evening, Guy waited for Piers as he was talking with Jan Hardy in the stables. Piers could see he had something on his mind.

'What is it, Guy?' he asked quietly.

'I don't like the situation. The King has stamped out of the castle. Half England knows that Clarence wishes to marry Isobel Neville and the King refuses his permissiion.'

'Do you think he loves her?'

'I expect so. She's a pretty little creature and if he doesn't love her he loves her money bags. Warwick is an extremely wealthy man and Isobel and Anne will share all his possessions at his death.'

Piers fell silent. He was thinking of Anne Neville.

'The devil of it is,' Guy continued soberly, 'Warwick is a fiend to cross. He is the Kingmaker and it is wise to remember that he could "unmake" kings, if he so desired.'

'Why should the King frown on this marriage?'

'He probably feels, and rightly so, that Warwick is already much too powerful. A daughter wedded into the Royal Family would increase his standing. Warwick, of course, has been out of favour since the King married Elizabeth Woodville.'

'What course do you think Gloucester till take?' Piers said, thoughtfully.

'The only one for him. You know his motto. "Loyaltie me Lie," Loyalty bindeth Me. He'll be true to Edward and the House of York.'

Piers watched Guy thoughtfully as he walked away. He knew only too well what such a choice of loyalty would cost his master.

CHAPTER SEVEN

When Piers and Guy Tremaine rode into the courtyard one morning, Jan Hardy came forward to take Piers's bridle rein. 'Can I have a word with you alone, Piers?' he said.

Piers followed the head groom into the shady coolness of the stable. Jan dismissed the other ostlers, then turned to face Piers.

'I have a message for you, lad. A groom from Warwick's household delivered it this morning and asked me to give it to you at the earliest possible moment.'

Piers broke the seal on the folded paper and turned to the light to see more easily. How he blessed Brother Martin's lessons, for he no longer needed a third person to read and tell him the letter's contents. It was very brief.

Piers,
   Once you told me I could rely on you if I needed help and I venture to ask for it now. I shall be at The Inn of the Golden Cockerel this afternoon. Unless you wish harm to come to me, tell no one in the household of this letter. Do not fail me.

Alicia.

He screwed it up and turned to face Jan.

'You can read it, Piers?'

'Yes, Jan, I can read it.'

'The messenger said I was to say to you, Alicia – the Golden Cockerel, this afternoon. That was in case you failed to read the note. On no account, he said, were you to ask any-one else to read it for you.'

'Can you have a horse ready for me this afternoon? I may need it to ride into the city.'

'Certainly, lad.'

'Thank you, Jan and . . . Jan . . . ' He turned in the door-

41

way, 'say nothing to anyone about this business.'

'You can trust me,' was the quiet rejoinder.

Guy gave him a curious glance, as they walked together to their quarters.

'How do I get permission to leave the castle?' Piers asked somewhat abruptly.

'You must ask the Duke.'

There was a little silence as they walked on and though Guy gave him another searching glance, he asked no questions. At length, Piers turned and faced him.

'I may have to go without permission,' he said, in a low voice.

'Be careful,' the other said, warningly. 'The Duke is no easy man to disobey.'

'I know, but my business is urgent.'

Guy shrugged philosophically.

'Anything I can do?'

Piers smiled faintly. 'Just make excuses for me if questions are asked.'

'I'll do my best.'

'I imagine I shall be back before I could be missed.'

'You'd better be, or I wouldn't be in your shoes for all the gold in the City Guild's treasury.'

Piers nodded, grinned and walked off to his own room.

Richard of Gloucester was seated on the lawn at the rear of the castle, when Piers sought him early that afternoon. He looked up with a faint smile at his squire's approach. 'I was about to send for you.'

'There is nothing wrong, sir?'

'If there is, I have not heard about it. No, I wished to see you about something more pleasurable. I see you wear the belt, which was your prize in last week's wager.'

'Yes, sir. Charles Beaumont gave it to me the same day.'

'Very commendable of him. It is not my custom to offer bribes to my servants, Piers, but I am not averse to rewarding good service when it is freely offered. The armourer came this morning and delivered this. I feel it will be quite comfortable in so fine a belt.'

Piers could not suppress a gasp of surprise as, from the grass by his side, the Duke bent and picked up an elaborately chased sword sheath. From it, he unsheathed the blade and held it out to the boy.

'Jehan tells me you know how to use it.'

Impulsively Piers kissed the hand which held it out to him. 'How can I thank you?'

'Promise me you will draw it only in self defence or in the service of your King. You are not to indulge in tavern brawls, Piers.'

'No, my lord.' Piers tried the blade. The hilt was workmanlike, but finely fashioned. He sheathed it and belted it on. 'Will you need me this afternoon, sir?'

'I don't think so, but stay within call. I am expecting a message from the King and may need you to ride with the answer.'

Piers walked away, a little uncertainly. He dare not ask for permission now. What was he to do? The Duke might send for him at any moment. On the other hand, he might not be required for another three or four hours. Alicia had said, 'Do not fail me.' How could he, when she really needed him? With good fortune he could be back in just over an hour.

For once, the streets of London held no attraction for Piers as he galloped impatiently through them.

At last he drew rein before the inn and gave his horse into the care of an ostler, bidding him have it ready, as he might wish to leave in a hurry. In the tap-room, Bess hurried to greet him with several gleaming tankards in either hand. One or two people glanced at him with marked respect, for he now wore the familiar device of a white boar on his tunic, the livery of the Duke of Gloucester.

'Piers,' Bess said warmly, 'I am glad to see you,' then in a lowered tone, 'she is upstairs in the front parlour.'

'I'll go straight up.'

'Shall I get you some food?'

'No, Bess. I dare not stay. I have duties and mustn't be missing when I'm needed.' Piers hurried up the stairs and entered the welcome coolness of the parlour. Alicia rose from a chair to greet him. She was wearing a riding cloak but the hood had slipped back from her shoulders. 'Oh Piers, you have come.'

'But of course. You said you needed me.'

She led him over to a settle and touched his brave new tunic with a smile. 'We were so glad to hear of your good fortune. You obtained permission to leave Baynards Castle?'

'Never mind that. Tell me you are not in trouble?'

'No.' She frowned and he took one of her hands within his own.

'Something *is* troubling you, Alicia. Tell me what it is.'

'I feel I have to tell someone, Piers. But I . . . I hardly know, even now, whether I ought to tell you. There is danger in it for someone . . . if not for you, because you know of it – for . . . ' Her voice broke off, then she resumed, looking away from him out of the window.

'I have really come to say goodbye, Piers.'

'You are leaving London?'

'Yes, all of us, the whole of the Warwick household. We go abroad, possibly to France.'

'France?' Piers's ejaculation expressed his astonishment. 'But why?'

'Can't you guess?' Her answer was breathlessly excited. 'Oh Piers, how can I tell you? I fear this journey. It spells discontent, anger, rebellion.'

Piers's eyes narrowed. 'Alicia, you must tell me all you know.'

She hesitated, but only for a moment. 'I have watched carefully. There has been constant coming and going of couriers; letters have passed. The whole household is in a ferment. My Lady the Countess weeps – and Clarence is never absent from My Lord's side.'

'When do you go? Do you know?'

'Tomorrow, very early.'

'How many men does Warwick take?'

'Near enough a hundred.'

He turned away, thoughtfully. 'You know of his destination?'

'I think, Calais.'

'There may be nothing in it. He has the command of Calias.'

'And takes his household? I tell you, Piers, there is more in it than that. Warwick is furious with the King. He feels slighted and wronged. Warwick *makes* kings and if they do not suit him, he will make others.'

'You think he would openly rebel against the King?'

'I think he goes to France to seek Margaret of Anjou.'

'She would have nothing to do with him. He was the cause of her defeat at Mortimer's Cross.'

'I'm not so sure. If she could be certain of Warwick's allegiance, she would make another attempt to gain the throne for the House of Lancaster.'

44

'Alicia, what are you saying?'

'I hardly know, Piers. I . . . what I am trying to explain is this. I love Warwick. He has treated me like a daughter. Anne and Isobel are to me as sisters. I would not bring him to death . . . but I feel you must be warned. Whatever happens, till death, I am faithful to the House of York.'

Piers walked to the window and stared out, his back to her, hands clasped behind him. When he spoke, his words were low and deliberate.

'What do you want me to do, Alicia? Inform the Duke? If I do, and your suspicions prove correct, it would mean the death of Warwick.'

'I know.' She wrung her hands together in a gesture of misery, so alien to her sunny nature. 'That is why I wanted to see you. I wanted your advice. I don't want to be the cause of Warwick's execution for treason.'

'Suppose Warwick was allowed to go out of the country – and then the Duke was warned? Would that suit the case?'

'It might. At any rate, I feel he should know of his brother's intending treachery.'

'That is very true.'

'Oh, Piers,' she said brokenly, 'what am I to do?'

'Alicia, I wish I could help you. I don't know what to advise you. Would you,' he paused, 'would you consider leaving Warwick's service and appealing to the King for protection?'

She shook her head emphatically.

'Where Anne Neville goes, I go. I will never leave her.'

Piers was about to reply when there came a soft tap on the door and Alicia placed a finger on her lip, in a warning gesture.

'Come in,' she called.

Jake Garnet came in, and seized the boy's hand in his own gigantic one, in a gesture of affectionate greeting.

'My lady,' he said quietly, 'you had best not stay too late.'

She rose and redonned her riding hood, hiding her luxuriant hair.

'I will take you home,' Piers said quickly.

'Not in that livery,' she answered with a slight smile. 'Jake will see me safe.'

'You will look after her,' Piers appealed to the innkeeper, who gave a great booming laugh.

'Well, bless you, lad, of course I will.'

Alicia held out her hand to him and Piers bent to kiss her slim white fingers.

'Goodbye, my lady. God bless you and her you serve,' he whispered softly.

At the door she turned back. 'Tell Gloucester the moment you think it necessary. I leave it to you to do what is right.'

He nodded briefly and then she was gone. He stood in the quiet little room and listened to her feet on the stairs, the soft rustle of her gown, the innkeeper's low voice bidding her take care and her soft sweet answer.

The ostler had his horse ready and in a matter of moments he was galloping hard along the London streets, fuming at every little hold-up he encountered. When at last he drew rein in the castle courtyard, he had been absent about an hour and a half. Jan Hardy himself hurried forward to take his horse. He was about to say something, when he stopped and gave Piers a warning glance. Piers turned and encountered the stern face of Jehan Treves, who had come up behind them. The moment he spoke, Piers knew that his worst fears were realised.

'Where have you been?' he demanded. 'The whole household has accompanied the Duke of Gloucester to Shene. We have been searching for you everywhere.'

'I . . . I went out into the city on business,' Piers faltered.

'The Duke is furious. You will be extremely lucky if he doesn't dismiss you from his service. As for your career as a squire,' he shrugged, meaningly. 'His Grace received an invitation from the King to join him at Shene on a hunting party and prepared to leave at once. He informed me that you were given instructions to hold yourself in readiness in case your services were required. You deliberately disobeyed the Duke's orders. You are to go to your room and continue with your studies until the Duke returns and decides what is best to be done with you.'

'But can I not go to Shene? I want to see the Duke.'

'No doubt,' Jehan retorted grimly, 'but for once you will do as you are told. Of course, you cannot go to Shene without the direct invitation of the King.'

'How long will he be gone, Jehan?'

'I really can't imagine.'

'But Jehan . . . '

The retainer turned and looked long and earnestly at Piers.

'If it were a matter of life and death, Piers, I would not advise you to disobey the Duke's orders for a second time. If you do, I will not answer for the consequences. You are left in my charge. You will work hard at your studies and in the exercise of arms and you are not, on any account, to leave the castle. No doubt, if you convince the Duke that a recurrence of this is not likely to happen again, he will perhaps, place you among my men-at-arms.'

'You don't think he will dismiss me altogether?'

'I don't know. The Duke will not have disobedience or laziness. On the other hand, I think, if he had intended to do so, he would have ordered me to dismiss you at once.'

Piers turned and walked away. He was almost blind with grief and shame. He stumbled up to his own little room and stared at a piece of parchment which lay on the chest. He picked it up and broke the seal. It was from Guy.

'Piers, I tried to cover your absence, but all to no avail. The Duke is furiously angry. I know you must have had an extremely good reason for absenting yourself. If the hunt is good and the King gracious, mayhap Gloucester will be merciful.'

Piers folded the letter and sat on the bed, gazing despondently at the floor. If he were dismissed Gloucester's service, he thought his heart would break and yet, as he considered Alicia's troubled brown eyes, usually so vivacious and alight with laughter, he knew that he could never have failed her. His thoughts thus turned to her warning. This apparently settled the matter. He must wait and hope Gloucester would not be long before he tired of the hunt. That prospect was hopeful, for the Duke's infirmity made it difficult for him to spend long hours in the saddle. With any luck, he might return before the end of the week and until then Piers must swallow his impatience as best he could.

CHAPTER EIGHT

On the fifth day of the Duke's absence, Piers sat dejectedly on the lawn when one of the ostlers came, pulled a forelock respectfully, and said, 'Jan says he has something important to say to you.'

Piers jumped to his feet eagerly. 'I'll come at once.' He found Jan outside the stable. He gave a brief nod in the direction of its cool interior.

'A man to see you. Says he must give his message to you and none other. He's in there.'

Piers thanked him and entered the stable. A man stepped out of the shadows. A shaft of sunlight fell across his face and with an exclamation of surprise, Piers recognised the thief who had attacked Alicia. The man smiled.

'I see you recognise me, young sir. I come for the sake of her who saved my life.'

'You may give me the message.'

'It is here, sir.' The man fumbled in his tunic and held out a letter folded and sealed. Piers turned away from him to the light and read its brief contents.

Piers,
    You will be interested to know that George and Bella, Having obtained permission from the Church, are to be married tomorrow. I am sorry you will not be able to attend, but the wedding will be somewhat hurried. No doubt you will inform Dickon.
                    From the hand of your sister,
                                    Alice.

He crumpled the letter violently in his hand. He hadn't a single doubt as to its meaning. In defiance of the King, Clarence intended to marry Warwick's daughter. The outcome of this could mean nothing but open rebellion, Gloucester must be informed at once. He nodded to the man and threw him a single silver piece.

'Do you return to your mistress?'

'Aye, young sir, at once.'

'You ran a risk to bring me this message.'

'I would run greater for her dear sake.'

Piers's eyes gleamed. 'Good man. Tell her all shall be done that can be done and give her my thanks. Now, off with you and God go with you.'

The man hurried out and Piers, dashing to the stable-door, yelled for Jan. The head groom came at once in answer to the summons.

'Jan – I want the finest horse in the stable. I ride at once to Shene.'

Hardy hesitated for just a fraction of a second, then he nodded and hastened off. Piers dashed across the courtyard and up to his room. He tore off his fine tunic with the badge of the white boar plainly emblazoned on it and chose to wear for the journey a plain homespun tunic of fustian he had worn during his period of service in the stables. Over this, he wore a dark riding cloak. He buckled on sword and dagger and thus armed, hurried out into the sunshine. Jan Hardy stood waiting, a high-bred, fast-moving chestnut by his side. He said nothing as Piers, tight lipped, sprang into the saddle.

'Tell Jehan I ride to Shene to seek Gloucester – tell him ... It's a matter of life and death.'

'Right. Take care of yourself, lad.'

Piers smiled, raised his hand in salute and then without further talk, he was off at full gallop.

It was late afternoon before he at length pulled his trembling mount to a halt before the King's favourite residence. Here Edward loved to escape the cramping duties of the court to hunt and ride. At the gateway, Piers was challenged.

'A courier, bringing urgent messages for his Grace of Gloucester,' he returned hurriedly in answer.

'Pass into the courtyard,' the sergeant-at-arms ordered, and he rode on. An ostler took his mount and at the door of the palace, a steward barred his way.

'I am the Duke of Gloucester's squire. I bring urgent news from London and must speak with him immediately,' he said, proudly tossing back his head.

The steward took in his dishevelled appearance, his dust-covered garments and wind-blown hair. It was plain that here was one on an errand of some importance. He summoned a young page.

'Take this boy to the Duke of Gloucester's apartments.'

Piers followed the boy through the corridors and they at last came to a halt before an oaken door. Piers hesitated. He dismissed the page, then summoning all his courage, knocked. A stern voice bade him enter. He squared his shoulders, then obeyed.

The Duke was discussing some plans with Sir Richard Ratcliffe. He looked up at the boy in the doorway and frowned angrily.

'Your Grace, please forgive this intrusion. I know you must be very angry with me – but I need private speech with you urgently.'

The frown on the Duke's brow deepened. 'How dare you? This is the second time you disobey my orders in the space of five days and then you have the insolence to ask my friend to leave so that you may proffer your explanations in private. I have no wish to listen to your excuses now or at any time.'

'My lord, I beg you, punish me any way you will, but please grant me five minutes with you alone. I have no excuse to offer. I have a matter of the gravest importance I wish to impart to you.'

Gloucester raised one eyebrow, expressively.

'Richard, do you mind leaving me for a few minutes? I feel I had best get to the root of this matter.'

Gloucester waited until the door closed and then said in an icy tone, 'Well?'

Piers waited for nothing. He plunged into his news at once.

'My Lord, Warwick has gone to Calais taking with him the Duke of Clarence and there your brother married the Lady Isobel Neville.'

'No.' The word was soft and yet so forceful that Piers could hardly believe his ears. 'No, he would not *dare* disobey the King.'

'Your Grace, I know it to be true,' Piers said quietly.

'Where did you get this information?'

'From Mistress Standish. She travelled to Calais in Warwick's household.'

'She sent you a message by courier?'

'Yes, Sir.'

50

'When?'

'This afternoon.'

Gloucester passed a hand wearily over his forehead. 'When did you first know about this?'

'I knew that Warwick had left for Calais on the day you left London, but I did not know then that the Duke of Clarence had joined him.'

'You gained that first information from Mistress Standish too, I take it?'

'Yes, your Grace. She sent me a note asking me to meet her. She begged me to tell no one in the castle about our meeting. That is why I left without asking you for permission. She seemed very distressed. She was sure that something more than a routine visit was afoot.'

'Go on.'

'Well, sir – she seemed to think Warwick was plotting to meet Margaret of Anjou.' Here Piers looked up at the Duke, but his expression remained unchanged, so he continued. 'She was very anxious to save the Earl's life. She owes him much.'

'Naturally.'

'And did not know what to do or whom to tell. Her sympathies are all with the House of York.'

'And what did *you* intend to do with the information?'

'Well, sir, to bide my time and then tell you.'

'I see. Who else knows of this?'

'No one, my lord, but myself.'

'What about the messenger?'

'He carried sealed papers, sir.'

Gloucester smiled grimly. He rose and limped over to the window, where he remained for some moments looking out, then he crossed to the table and rang a small handbell. Piers watched him anxiously and cleared his throat, nervously.

'My lord,' he pleaded, 'you will be merciful. Don't dismiss me from your service. I will work in the stables, my lord, and I will never disobey you, I swear it.'

'Unless Mistress Standish calls,' interrupted the Duke coldly. Piers hung his head. To that, he had nothing to say in answer. At that moment, the door opened and Guy Tremaine entered. Seeing Piers, he started, violently.

'Oh, it's you Guy. Good, it *is* you I wanted. Now listen carefully. When the King returns from hunting, go to him, give my regards and beg him to give me a private audience.

Impress upon him that my business is urgent.'

'Yes, your Grace.'

'And Guy . . . ' the Duke arrested the boy as he prepared to leave the room. 'Whoever is with the King, even if it is the Queen herself, I rely on you to get me that interview.'

'Yes, my lord.' Guy threw Piers a look of sympathy, bowed respectfully to the Duke and withdrew.

'And now, Piers,' the Duke turned to the boy, who stood dejectedly silent, waiting. 'We come back to you and the subject of your disobedience. On consideration, I will not dismiss you. I will consider later what punishment to impose.'

Piers stared at him joyfully.

'Then I may work again with Jan Hardy?'

'No. You will continue as my squire.'

Piers's face paled with the suddenness of his joy.

'It is not out of consideration for you, but I fear I shall need a well-trained squire in battle, not a raw youth.'

'Then you think it will come to that?'

Again the Duke sighed heavily. 'You are no longer a child and no fool. You must realise what this means.' He seated himself and tapped an impatient finger on the table. 'I hope the King is not long. When I get that interview, I wish you to tell His Grace all you know, you understand?'

'Yes, sir.'

'Go now and make yourself presentable. If Sir Richard Ratcliffe is waiting, tell him to return to me.'

As Piers opened the door, the Duke called him back.

He recrossed the room and stood once more by his master's chair. 'I have not yet thanked you. You ran a great risk this afternoon.'

'No greater than Alicia, when she wrote the message, sir.'

'No, Mistress Standish is a brave girl and a resourceful one. We owe you both our grateful thanks.'

'Then, in time, you will forgive me, my lord?'

The Duke smiled, slightly. 'Yes, I suppose so,' he said quietly. 'Now go, lad, and do my bidding.'

By sunset, the King had still not returned to the Palace. The Duke moved restlessly about his apartment. Time was an important factor now. Sir Franics Lovell and Sir Richard Ratcliffe sat in a corner playing chess.

'Patience, Dickon,' said Sir Francis, smilingly, 'you know Edward will not give up the chase till it is too dark to see.'

The Duke made no answer and the two companions exchanged meaning glances. Silently they continued their game. Piers sat on a stool in the darkening room, watched the three and waited. An hour passed. There was no sound from the courtyard outside. Soon the candles would have to be lit. Richard sank despondently into a chair and stared dejectedly ahead.

Half an hour later there came a noise of stamping, the jingling of harness and grooms hurried out to take the horses. The courtyard flared with lighted brands. The King had returned. Duke Richard did not move. Even now it would be difficult to get a word with him. He would be tired and hungry, unwilling to discuss business. The Woodvilles would surround him with their witty, senseless talk and try everything possible to keep him from his brother's side. At that moment Guy tapped and entered.

'The King's Grace will see you after dinner, your Grace.'

'Is Lord Scales with him?'

'Yes, sir, at least, he was a moment ago.'

'Good lad. You have done well.' The Duke nodded, well satisfied. 'And now, gentlemen, into dinner.'

The King did not dine in the Great Hall and was obviously resting in his private apartments. The meal over, Duke Richard called Piers to his side and the two went together to the King's suite of rooms. A page announced them and Gloucester limped impatiently into his brother's presence.

The King leaned back upon the silken cusions of a daybed and yawned indolently. 'Well, Dickon,' he said, lightly, 'suppose you sit down and tell me this matter that is so important that it cannot wait until morning. Can you not see how tired I am?'

The Duke ignored the invitation to sit, but stood, looking down at his brother with troubled grey eyes. 'This is the crux of the matter. George has gone off to Calais with Warwick and married Isobel.'

The lazy body stiffened very slightly. 'You jest, Brother,' he said, in the same, slow even tones.

'I was never so serious in my life.'

'But how do you know?'

'My squire told me.'

The King threw back his head and gave peal after peal of laughter. 'Oh, Dickon,' he said, 'I thought better of you.

53

You listen to a squire's tale. They gossip like fishwives.'

'I would trust Piers with my life,' the Duke interrupted steadily, 'and lay my Dukedom as wager on his trustworthiness and honesty.'

'But I don't understand . . . How does he know?'

'Piers,' the Duke called the boy forward, 'tell His Grace everything you know about this affair.'

Piers came forward and knelt before the King, who sat up and nodded to him, more briskly now.

'All right, Boy, stand up and don't be nervous. Tell me quickly.'

Piers told the King everything Alicia had told him and how he had ridden to Shene with the news. All traces of laziness left the King and, as the story proceeded, a dark frown gradually formed on the royal brow. At the close of the narrative, he jumped to his feet and prowled angrily round the room.

'How dare he?' he shouted. 'How dare he sneak off with Warwick and defy me behind my back? I forbade this marriage. I'll arrest both of them. Warwick shall go the Tower and George with him. A murrain. Can a man not trust his own flesh and blood?'

The Duke followed his brother's angry pacing with his eyes, then he limped to a seat and sat down. Piers drew back and waited until summoned. The King moved restlessly to and fro, striking a clenched fist smack against his hand and uttering dark threats against his rebellious subject and treacherous brother, then, meeting Richard's steady gaze, he broke off and sighed heavily.

'What am I to do?'

'There isn't anything you can do. The Pope has granted a dispensation and I feel convinced they are already married. Why you should have been so hot against the marriage I can't imagine. You have angered Warwick needlessly by your refusal to give consent to it, and he is an awkward man to cross. The best thing is to attempt to win back his friendship.'

'What, after he had played me false?'

'You can ill afford to do otherwise. A quarrel with Warwick would mean civil war.'

'Then what do you suggest I do?'

'We must return to London to inspect your fortifications.'

'We'll ride at once . . . '

'Nay, spare me that,' the Duke said quietly, 'that can wait

until the morning. We are all in need of a night's rest.'

The King was silent for a moment, then he gave in. 'As usual, you are right. We all need the rest. We ride at dawn. Do you come with me, Dickon?'

'Of course.'

'Thank you,' the King said simply. The Duke rose and, as he moved to the door, the King recalled him. 'We owe something to your squire. Speak, boy. What favour can I grant you?'

Piers flushed hotly and glanced up at Gloucester. 'Why nothing, Sire. I desire nothing but my lord's . . . ' Here he broke off and then, stealing a shy glance at his master, said quickly, 'There is one favour you could grant me, Sire. Beg my Lord Duke to forgive me.'

'Forgive you?' the King's eyebrows shot up in an interrogatory expression. 'For what?'

'For my disobedience, sire.'

'I see.' The King's lips twitched slightly and he looked gravely at his brother. 'Will you forgive him, for my sake, Dickon?' he said wistfully. 'After all, if he had not been disobedient, we should have had no warning at all.'

Gloucester looked down at his squire sardonically, 'Perhaps not. As Your Grace wishes, of course.'

The next morning, the King was up at dawn and the whole household prepared to return to London. For once, Gloucester rode with the King at the head of the line, a place of honour usually held by the Queen's relatives, but today Edward wanted his brother near him for advice and comfort. Piers rode with Guy and the two had much to talk about. Already the news of Clarence's marriage had leaked out and was the chief subject of conversation in the Royal Household. Piers forbore to comment. Guy gloomily prophesied war.

'Here's your chance to win your spurs and get it over with,' Piers grinned.

Part of Guy's gloomy foreboding came true, for one morning when Guy and Piers, with their respective masters, were at the Tower, the news came in that rebellion had broken out in the north. There had been some fighting, during which the Queen's father and brother had been killed. The Queen was distracted and the King almost too worried to be able fully to comfort her. Gloucester decided to leave the Palace and return at once to Baynards Castle. The household seemed to be in ferment and he felt he must have, for a while, the peace and momentary security of his own house.

He rode straight into the courtyard, nodded curtly to the groom who took his horse and limped to his own apartments. Piers followed and was engaged in various small tasks when a knock came at the door. Gloucester motioned him to answer it. The Duchess of York stood there, her face deadly pale. She brushed by Piers and went to her son, who rose at once to greet her.

'Dickon, Warwick has landed at Winchelsea. George is with him.' Her face contorted suddenly and the Duke, concerned, led her to a chair.

'Dear heart, do not concern yourself. Who knows why he comes?'

'Dickon, I am afraid.'

The Duke smiled reassuringly. 'Why should you fear?'

'Go to George. Beg him to return to Edward and make his peace.'

Gloucester stared at her for a moment without speaking. She held out her hands imploringly. 'Is it not enough that I lose a husband and one son in these wars? Must I lose other sons too? Please, Dickon, you will go?'

The Duke forced a smile. 'Aye, madam, if you wish it. Now go, rest.' He placed an arm round her shoulders and led her from the room. Piers gazed ruefully at the clothes he had been putting away. When the Duke returned, he asked simply, 'Do we go at once, sir?'

'We go at once. Order the horses.'

An hour later, they were once more on the road.

CHAPTER NINE

Piers leaned back on the grass and yawned wearily. The last few weeks had certainly been hard. There they were at last in Doncaster and, in his opinion, lucky to be quartered here, in this fine house, instead of in a tent on the battlefield. Guy's voice droned on steadily and Piers turned over on to his stomach and tried to sleep. Sleep evaded him and his mind turned on the events of the past weeks. In spite of very hard riding, Gloucester and he had failed to catch the rebel lords at Winchelsea. They had, by a mishap, taken a wrong turning and failed to meet up with Warwick. Tired and almost fainting in the saddle, Gloucester had been forced to halt at a small wayside inn and rest. Piers too, had reached the limit of his endurance and the two had slept for almost twelve hours. Then, once refreshed, they had immediately taken the road to London once more.

At Baynards Castle they heard the news. Warwick, now a declared rebel, had gone to Shene and taken the King prisoner. He was now at his own castle, Middleham, the King helpless in his hands. Piers remembered the white face of the Duchess, as she related the news to her youngest son. Grim-lipped, Gloucester rode to Middleham, accompanied by his friends, Lovell and Ratcliffe, and there had demanded from Warwick the release of the King.

Bitter words were exchanged. Richard quarrelled hotly with his brother George, but for a time the breach was healed and Edward reigned again in Westminster, but after three months, Warwick, smarting under some slight, imagined or fancied, went to France in a fury accompanied by the still faithful Clarence. Three days later Gloucester received his greatest blow.

During all this time, Piers had heard and seen nothing of Alicia. Warwick kept the ladies of his household away from the court and, try as he might, it had proved impossible for Piers to catch a glimpse of her. When Warwick prepared to leave the court for the second time, he sent his family on ahead and it was not until later that Alicia was able to send her messenger to Piers.

Will Rawlings brought the news, as he had before, but this time it was so serious in content that it was decided it was too dangerous for him to rejoin his mistress and even now he worked in the Duke's service.

Alicia wrote,

Things have progressed from bad to worse. The quarrel between Margaret and our uncle has finally been patched up and the two have decided to go into business together. To seal the agreement, Anne has become betrothed to young cousin Edward. My fondest love to you, dear brother.

Alice.

Piers had crumpled the letter in his hand and gone in search of his master. The Duke was in his room reading.

'Why so grim, my squire?'

'I have bad news, sir. From Mistress Standish.'

'What is it, Piers?' he asked quietly.

For answer, the boy held out the letter and the room was deadly quiet as the Duke perused its brief contents. He carried it to the fire which was burning on the open hearth, for in spite of the autumn sunshine the room was chilly and now it seemed to Piers, standing there, that it had become even more so. The Duke remained silent, though Piers noticed the ominous tightening of his lips, then he stooped quickly and dropped the missive on to the fire, watched it burn for a moment, then nodded simply.

'Thank you. As you say, it is bad news. In fact I doubt if it could be worse. The King must be informed at once and we will confer what is best to be done. Go, get Jan to saddle my horse and, Piers, don't gossip about this to anyone.'

'No, sir. May I accompany you?'

'If you wish.'

Anne Neville betrothed to Edward, Prince of Wales, the heir to the Lancastrian house. Could this news indeed be worse? Warwick made no further attempts to hide his treachery. He was now openly allied to Margaret of Anjou and the Lancastrian cause.

Disaster followed disaster. Warwick landed and the country folk flocked to his banner. The King left London, accompanied by the Duke of Gloucester, and here they were encamped in Doncaster. London had fallen to the Kingmaker and there he openly avowed Henry of Lancaster to be the rightful King and Edward of York a usurper. Piers had heard that King Henry had been fetched out of the Tower by Warwick and paraded through the streets for everyone to see.

Guy continued to grumble and Piers climbed unwilling to his feet. 'Come, let's go for a walk.'

Still complaining Guy clambered to his feet and followed his companion out of the gate.

The town was filled to overflowing with men-at-arms wearing the livery of their respective masters. The presence of the King in Doncaster had attracted groups of pedlars, who displayed their wares to the soldiers, who were anxious to buy trinkets for their sweethearts at home. They stopped for an idle moment or two to watch the antics of a dancing bear and were most impressed by the difficult feats performed by a travelling juggler.

'Let us go to market,' Guy suggested. 'I would like to buy some small gift for my sister, Margaret.'

Piers readily agreed. Guy soon recovered his customary good humour and stopped to stare in various shops as they passed. He finally purchased a tiny golden locket, simple but delicately contrived, after a good deal of shrewd bargaining.

There was a crowd in the open market-place. Country girls and yokels had come into the town bearing eggs and fresh vegetables for sale, as the army needed large supplies. Probably some quack doctor was attempting to persuade them to buy a marvellous elixir guaranteed to cure every ailment or mayhap a sword swallower was entertaining the crows. Whatever it was, it was attracting attention, for every moment the throng grew in density. Piers and Guy pressed steadily nearer, but even after standing on tip-toe and attempting to infiltrate farther into the centre, they found it impossible to see over the heads and the crowds closed in and, try as they may, they were unable to penetrate further.

'Can you hear what is happening?' Guy asked, as they were thrown suddenly against one another.

'Not a thing,' Piers said, 'I think someone's haranguing the crowd, but I'm not sure.'

There was a good deal of pushing and shouting, and then a sudden hush fell upon the gathering.

'Why should you support a coward and usurper? How does this puppet King, Edward, treat those who serve him? Does he reward them? No, I tell you he surrounds himself with fools and cravens. He lazes in the Palace of Westminster, which is the rightful home of our sovereign lord, King Henry VI, God bless him.'

Guy stared at Piers, his face strained and white. 'Treason,' he whispered hoarsely, 'we must get to the King.'

'No, wait,' Piers restrained him, with a hand on his arm and strained his ears to listen to the remainder of this rebellious speech.

'And now, my friends, this coward and usurper has come here to Doncaster, to quarter his men in your houses and you will starve while his armies feed. To arms, men of Doncaster. Support your rightful King, Harry and the red rose of Lancaster.'

'Aye, aye, he's right.' There was a surge forward and a thousand hands were up to support the speaker's arrogant assertion. To his horror, Piers realised that the crowd was being swayed, and that right easily, against the King. The speaker's voice dropped to scarce above a whisper and yet so had he managed to get the crowd on his side that every word he said carried.

'Let us, my friends, take this King unawares. Warwick the Kingmaker will be truly grateful, that I promise you . . .'

Piers waited to hear no more. He attempted to wiggle clear of the crowd. This was by no means easy, but when it was at last accomplished he found his arm caught in an urgent clasp and Guy spoke softly in his ear.

'Come, Piers, let us go into the tailor's shop. We need warm cloaks and I am told he has an excellent selection.'

Piers stared at him in amazement. 'Can you think of mantles at such a time?'

Guy's grip tightened suddenly and he said, urgently, 'Don't argue now, Piers. Do as I say. Make for that shop.' He indicated a small draper's shop to the right of the market-place and with a slight movement of his hand on Piers's arm, guided him in that direction. Wonderingly, Piers stumbled after him. Once clear of the crowd, Guy whispered in his ear, 'careful, yon fellow in the grey tunic has his eyes on us. We must try to give him the slip.'

'But we have no time,' Piers hissed back, 'we must warn the King and at once.'

'First we must *get* to the King,' his friend cautioned softly, 'and we won't, if we don't take care. Did you see who was responsible for the rising of the townsfolk?'

Piers nodded. 'Yes, the Marquis of Montecute, Warwick's brother.'

'Aye, the King was a fool to put his trust in a Neville. That fellow is one of his creatures. They will try to prevent us from warning the King. We are most conspicuous in this livery. We must try and get something to cover our tunics. Come.'

Without further argument, Piers followed him across the market-place and into the darkened recess of the shop. He understood at once the wisdom of Guy's remarks. Guy went to the counter and began to bargain with the young apprentice. Piers sauntered to the back of the shop as casually as possible to weigh up the chances of making an exit that way. They seemed good. The doorway led into a back parlour which was uninhabited. Behind, Piers glimpsed the open doorway into the courtyard. His sense of direction told him that an alley led to the backs of all these shops. Here, then, was their way. They must rush through the back of the shop, climb the wall and drop into the alley. From there, they would be able to make their way, as unobtrusively as possible, to the castle. He turned back to the counter.

Guy had apparently completed his haggling and was paying for two drab-coloured mantles, which he bore over his arm.

'Aye, sir,' the sandy-haired apprentice was saying, ' 'tis true, if there is fighting and the way things are going, 'tis bound to come to it, you'll need warm cloaks.'

Piers beckoned to Guy, who thanked the lad and crossed to his side. Piers pointed and spoke swiftly. 'Quick, this way.'

Guy did not stop to argue. The two made a dash through the private parlour. Behind, in the shop, they heard the lad's startled shout, 'Hey – you can't go that way. Come back, Sirs . . . '

Neither stopped to look behind him. In a moment, they were out of the house and running across the cobbled courtyard. Guy hurled the cloaks headlong over the wall into the alley beyond and then began to tear off his silken tunic.

'Get rid of your tabard here,' he said and Piers hastily followed suit.

Both were excellent climbers and, panting for breath, they stayed but for a second on top of the wall to look beneath. No one was in sight. Piers jumped and landed lightly. He clambered to his feet instantly and gave a hand to Guy who had slipped forward on to his knees and was cursing softly under his breath.

'All right?' Piers queried.

'Yes, perfectly, come on.'

They picked up a cloak each and covered their garments, then began to hurry down the alley. The streets seemed deserted, not a soul in sight.

'They must be all at the rally in the market-place,' Guy muttered uneasily. 'The King hasn't a chance. He must ride for the coast, at once.'

'He'll take some persuading, if I know anything of him,' Piers replied, breathlessly.

Once or twice they looked behind them, but no one seemed to notice them, and at last they saw the battlements of the fortified house, which Edward had commandeered for his headquarters in the city, rise before them. The two broke into a run and dashed through the gates.

'Close the gates,' Piers gasped to the sergeant-at-arms on guard. 'There is to be an attack. We go to warn the King.'

The man gaped at him wonderingly and Piers pushed impatiently past him.

'Fool, guard the gate. If that falls, all is lost.' He slithered to a halt and turned to confer with Guy.

'I'll go to the stables and get the horses saddled,' Guy said. 'You go straight to the King and try to persuade him to fly.'

Piers made a wry face, nodded and then they parted, on their different errands.

The King was at meat with the Duke of Gloucester and several of his friends when Piers burst into his presence. He ran to the table and knelt before him.

'Your Grace,' he panted, 'Montecute has raised the city by treachery for his brother, the Earl of Warwick. Even now, the townsfolk are mustering for an attack. Guy and I happened to be in the market-place and we tore on ahead to warn you.'

Gloucester sprang to his feet and limped to the window.

'A murrain,' he growled menacingly. 'Why did we trust a Neville?'

Already the sound of shouting and marching feet could be heard in the distance. The King sat for a moment as though stunned. Rivers and Lovell joined the Duke at the window.

'Warn the garrison to man the gates,' Rivers said, making for the staircase. The King roused himself and shouted for his squire.

'Haste boy, my harness,' he bawled. 'By God, I'll hold this house if it be the last thing I do in this life.'

The Duke turned a haggard face to his brother.

'No, Edward,' he said quietly, 'this time, discretion is the better part of valour. We must fly.'

Angry veins stood out on the King's forehead. 'Do you speak to me of flight?' he shouted. 'God's death, I fight and win or die fighting. No, brother, I'll not run like a fox at the first sound of the hunting horn.'

'You are the King. If you are killed our cause is lost,' Richard reasoned coolly. 'We have no chance here. Our position is hopeless. We have less than a score of men-at-arms in the house. We are taken by surprise. Listen to that mob.' He moved clumsily from the window and placed a slight, slim hand on his brother's shoulder. 'Truly, Edward, I counsel flight.'

'And I, sire,' Lovell said, quietly. Piers touched the Duke on the arm urgently.

'Guy has gone to see the horses saddled, sir. All is ready for flight.'

All unarmed, the King stood, feet astride, his face mottled with angry colour, sword drawn in his hand. 'I am tricked,' he said, between his teeth. 'One day I'll get even with Warwick for this treachery and George, my noble brother. I should never have left London.'

'Come, sire,' Ratcliffe urged, 'while there is yet time.'

The Duke touched his brother on the shoulder. 'Come, Edward,' he said quietly, 'these noble men risk their lives awaiting you.'

The King sighed heavily, then nodded and followed the others below stairs. Piers stumbled on ahead, to where Guy, white-faced, waited with the horses. The attack on the main gate had already begun, as the King and the handful of faithful knights who followed him mounted and rode through the back way. Here they were met by a small force of Montecute's men.

Gloucester and Lovell cut down two men, as they tried to prevent the King leaving. Rivers stayed behind to hold the gate and the others surged ahead. The little party rode like the wind, Piers and Guy finding it difficult to keep pace with them.

After about half an hour of this killing pace, they slackened rein a little, out of consideration for their mounts, and, as there seemed no sign of pursuit, the King held up his hand in a commanding gesture and the little troupe came to a halt. The King dismounted and went to his brother. 'Dismount and rest for a while, Dickon,' he said. 'We'll wait here for Rivers to join us – if he can. Rest now, snatch your opportunity while you may. Doubtless, we shall be in the saddle all day.'

Piers hurried forward to help his master. The Duke obeyed the King, dismounted and stretched himself out on a grassy slope. Most of the group followed his example. The King walked restlessly to and fro. No one said very much. Everyone felt dejected at this sudden defeat. It seemed to them all, though they dare not voice the thought, that here was an end of the House of York.

The silence in the little copse was broken by the sound of hoof beats coming quickly towards them. The Duke sat up and the expressions of all of them became charged with expectancy. The King ceased his pacing and stood listening intently, straining his ears in the direction of the sound. Then suddenly the rider came into sight and, looking at them, burst into a booming laugh. It was Earl Rivers, his clothes dirty and torn but his customary good humour unchanged.

'You are unhurt, Anthony?' the King said, hurrying forward to embrace him.

'Not a scratch.' He stretched himself on the ground and gratefully drank from a flask of water, which Lord Hastings held out to him. 'Ah, that's better.' He wiped his mouth and smiled up at the frowning company.

'How did you find us?' Gloucester inquired, in a harsh tone.

'That wasn't difficult. I followed the trail you blazed.'

The Duke nodded briefly and climbed to his feet. 'I feared as much. Do you hear that, Edward? We must move and make some effort to cover our tracks.'

The King nodded. 'You are right, Dickon. We'll wait until Lord Rivers has rested awhile, then we must be off.'

'Never mind me,' Rivers laughed. 'I'm fresh enough. Where are we going?'

'To the coast of course,' Gloucester snapped, impatiently.

'The nearest port is Bishops Lynn, but it's fully a day's riding,' Lord Lovell remarked.

'We'll make it,' the Duke replied curtly, 'though how we shall pay our passage, I've no idea. We took nothing of value in our flight.'

'I have only the clothes I stand in,' the King agreed, 'but I have this jewelled chain and my rings.'

'We must raise the money somehow and make for Holland. Once there, Burgundy will help us,' Gloucester said quietly, rising and moving towards his mount. The Duke of Burgundy was married to Edward's sister, Margaret, and would, they hoped, prove a useful ally.

They rode all that day, keeping close and as silent as possible. Twice, two of the knights left the group and returned a short time later with simple provisions, purchased from a nearby farmhouse. When it became too dark to ride farther, they dismounted and slept under the shelter of a small copse.

The following day dawned fair and the little group rode on. The Duke seemed haggard and dejected, but Rivers was his usual witty self and the King seemed to be regaining his good spirits. Just outside Bishops Lynn, they drew rein and held a short conference.

'It would be unwise for us to spend unnecessary time on the quay,' Gloucester said, practically. 'We ought to be reasonably sure of a passage, so that we can go on board immediately, before our presence arouses undue comment from the locals. I suggest someone goes ahead and interviews any captain he may find, arrange the crossing, then return later for us.'

'That sounds sense,' Rivers agreed. 'It had better not be anyone too well known.'

Piers drew nearer and touched the Duke's arm gently.

'I could go, my lord. None would notice me.'

'No indeed. I will allow no boy to take the risk,' the King retorted, firmly.

Gloucester stood still for a moment, looking thoughtfully down at Piers, then he nodded.

'Yes, I think perhaps you are right, Piers,' he said turning to the King. 'No one would notice a stripling and he can speak uncouthly if he is questioned.'

The King was still inclined to argue, but his brother drew him aside and, after a little whispering, he came back to the group and somewhat reluctantly gave his consent to the venture. Guy stepped forward, a little flushed, 'I may go too, sir?'

Gloucester turned and looked enquiringly at Sir Francis Lovell. 'What say you, Frank? I think they are safe enough.'

Sir Francis nodded briefly and Guy stood back with a sigh of relief. Gloucester called Piers to him and removed a ring from his finger. 'I want you to be cautious. You will need this for purposes of bribery, but don't go flashing it about before everyone you meet. Try to arrange a passage for all of us by the next tide, anywhere so long as we get the King out of the country. Remember, if it is humanly possible, we wish to conceal all knowledge of the King's presence here until the moment we are ready to leave.'

'I realise that, your Grace. You can trust me.'

'Right, then off you go. We will wait here under the trees.'

Still wrapped in their plain mantles, the two boys set off into the small port. They stopped at a pastrycook's shop and bought a quantity of food for the party, their share of which they ate almost at once. Then, without losing any more time, Piers made for the harbour. There were but three ships at anchor, all equally small and equally grimy. He looked at Guy and shrugged his shoulders. Small boats plied between the vessels and the landing stage and raucous voices were lifted in song from a dirty waterside tavern on the quay. The two boys picked their way through bales of wool and bundles of hides and stood at length looking out to sea.

An old sailor leaned forward over the wall and spat deliberately into the water. Piers glanced meaningly at Guy and sidled towards him. 'Fine ships,' he remarked, looking out to the three at anchor.

'Ay, fine vessels, for them as is fond of the sea, young master, but to others – why, they be but precarious wooden tubs and uncomfortable tubs too, specially in a storm.'

'I know it,' Piers said and sighed.

'You've been to sea, young master?'

'No indeed, I would, if I had half a chance, but my parents are set against it. They apprenticed me to a draper.'

The old sailor nodded slowly as an expression of sympathy.

'Where are they bound?' Piers remarked, casually.

'Well now, two of 'em ain't bound nowhere, leastways not yet. *The Beauty of Bridesmead*,' he indicated the farthest ship with a motion of his hand, 'she is my son's ship and they'll stay in harbour another week. Now the *Nancy*, she's in for repairs. Ran into a gale she did last trip and won't be seaworthy for at least another week.'

Piers's heart sank, as he stared down over the sparkling water, 'And the other?' he asked.

'Ahr, that be a different matter, young master, she is a Dutch ship, bound for Amsterdam, so I 'eard.'

'Does her captain speak English?'

The old man turned and looked at him, thoughtfully. 'Aye, Captain Van de Meer be able to talk the King's English, but mind, the sea be a hard life and if . . .'

Piers smiled and held out a coin. 'Thank you for your advice. I'll consider it.'

The sailor reached out a gnarled brown hand and took the coin, then he touched his forelock, respectfully. 'Cap'n Van de Meer be in yonder tavern. He's a small, pale-faced man 'as wears long gold ear-rings and 'as a black beard.'

'Thanks, good friend,' Piers said and moved off.

'What now?' Guy murmured urgently. Piers chuckled.

'Bless the old salt. He thinks we are planning to run away to sea. He's right in a way. Now to find Van de Meer.' He halted, as a small man came towards them out of the nearest tavern. He was bearded and wore dangling gold ear-rings. His rolling gait betrayed him as a seaman.

'Am I speaking to Captain Van de Meer?' Piers asked.

The seaman stood still, hand on hip, and glared down at the two boys.

'And if you are?' he rasped in a guttural, foreign voice.

'Then I would discuss business with you, sir.'

'You're an insolent young coxscomb and what manner of business would that be?'

'That, I would explain in private, sir.'

The sailor turned and led the way into the tavern. He went over to the landlord, who looked back at the boys, when finally led the three of them into the privacy of the back parlour. The Dutch captain flung himself down on a wooden chair and looked up at them. Piers wasted no time.

'My master and several friends desire to cross to Amsterdam

67

today. They are prepared to pay well for the passage.'

'How well?' the answer was swift and blunt. 'I'm a poor seaman, my young friend. Today is no day for the crossing. There's a storm blowing up. 'Tis a rough passage we'll have. If I'm to risk my ship it will have to be to some purpose.'

Piers held up Gloucester's ring. 'My master sends this as an earnest of his good faith.'

The man's eyes narrowed. 'I see. Why are they in such haste to cross?'

'They have their reasons.'

The sailor made no effort to take the ring. He stared over Piers's head for a moment, then suddenly, stood up. 'I'll take you. Get back to your master. Tell him to hurry. We'll be out on the tide in three hours, and warn him, I've no cabin and soft beds. He'll have to rough it and stay on deck with the cargo.'

'That, I am sure, will be understood,' Piers said, quietly, then he wrapped his cloak around him and the two left the tavern.

They regained their horses from the stable where they had left them, and rode back to the royal party. The King stood by Gloucester's side, angrily slapping his gauntlet against his thigh. Guy began to distribute the food they had bought and Piers crossed to the royal brothers and dropped on to his knee.

'I have passage on a Dutch ship, bound for Amsterdam on the next tide. She is the only ship fit to leave port, sire.'

'Good lad,' Gloucester's eyes gleamed with relief. 'Were questions asked?'

'I spoke to no one but an old sailor and he, I'm sure, thinks I'm a runaway to sea.'

Duke Richard's hand gripped his shoulder in a gesture of approval. 'Good. Now we must move, gentlemen, at once, for we have little time before the next tide.'

Captain Van de Meer was superintending the loading of provisions on the quay when Piers and the small party rode up. The King went straight over to him and held him in earnest conversation for some minutes. Piers saw the captain look over his tall, handsome figure and he smiled.

'I suggest you come aboard at once, sire, you and your party,' he said, quietly.

Swiftly the little group embarked into the boats until only Gloucester, Lovell and Guy and Piers were left on the landing stage. The Duke turned away and looked out to sea.

'Piers,' he said, slowly, 'you would be quite safe here in England. Your fortune is here, boy. Here we take leave of each other.'

'My lord, you do not mean it?' Piers whispered.

'Lad, I can offer you nothing in Holland. Who knows how long we shall be in exile, perhaps for ever. Jake Garnet will give you employment. If I return, you may re-enter my service again. The King and I have little money. We must rely on charity now.'

'You really wish me to stay?' Piers asked steadily.

The Duke turned and looked at him, but said nothing. 'You do not really wish me to leave you?' Piers repeated wistfully. Still the Duke said nothing. Piers saw the small boat approaching, heard it grind against the wall. In less than a minute, Gloucester would be gone from him. He heard the sailor's voice.

'Ready, my lord, I'll steady her for you.'

The Duke turned, a slight smile on his youthful lips. 'Down you go first, Piers,' he said. 'Then you can give me a hand. You are used to this confounded infirmity of mine.'

CHAPTER TEN

It was a cold blustery day in March when Piers first saw England again. He stood on deck and watched the grey coast-line slowly emerge from the mists and knew, with a sudden surging within his heart, gladness at being home. Gloucester and Lovell stood by the rail and he knew that the Duke was murmuring a fervent prayer for victory, for he saw him cross himself devoutly, before turning. Here it was at last, the chance for which they had waited so long, the opportunity for a final battle with Warwick for the throne. After long months in exile as the guests of the King's sister, Margaret, who was Duchess of Burgundy, her husband, the Duke, had at last provided Edward with the necessary money and ships.

It had been a frightful voyage. The King had insisted on embarking, in spite of the storm. They had delayed too long, he had said, and in the end the knights who were attempting to advise him gave up the struggle and the little fleet set sail for England. Guy was sick and still in the cabin. Piers hurried down to him and grinned as his friend turned over with a groan.

'Come on,' he said, 'it's much calmer now. We have sighted England.'

'Thank God and St Christopher,' said Guy feelingly, as he forced himself into a sitting posture. 'At last we shall be on dry land again. I tell you truly, Piers, I thought never to land alive. Oh, God, how ill I was.' He shuddered at the remembrance and turned away. 'Well, this determines it. Never will I put to sea again. If we lose this battle, I shall be captured and die by sword or rope, for I tell you, nothing would tempt me to brave this journey again.'

'Nonsense,' laughed his companion. 'You weren't ill going. It was that ghastly storm. Half the men were sick. The ship tossed from side to side and several times I thought those mountainous waves would wash right over the masts, but it's

70

much better now, though there's still a gale blowing.'

'Where are we landing?'

'I don't know. The original plan was Norfolk, but I fear we've been blown right off course. There's no sign of the other division.'

The little fleet had been divided into two, the King in command of the first division, and the Duke of Gloucester the second. The plan was for the two parties to meet and, come what may, march towards London. Both boys sprang to attention as the Duke was heard rather clumsily descending the ladder to the cabin. He was talking to Lovell, who followed.

'I shall land at the first suitable spot. While we are still at half strength, it would be rank stupidity to attempt a landing at one of the main ports. We can put ashore in the boats and make camp. Then I shall send out scouts to find the position of the King's force. Once we have joined up with the main party, I challenge any to attack.'

He turned and smiled grimly. 'Come, Piers, arm me, we must be prepared for all eventualities now.'

About two hours later one half of the Yorkist army landed on the sandy beaches of Goole. Guy and Piers were together in the fourth boat and Piers was greatly amused by Guy's anxiety to reach the shore. He scrambled out of the boat and waded to the beach, the water washing to his waist. Piers helped the boatmen pull the little craft clear of the waves and followed the party inland. Gloucester stood quite still on the beach, his eyes searching the hills and valleys of his beloved Yorkshire. He was home. Piers saw his lips tighten meaningly and knew his grim determination to stay, cost what it may.

None hindered them in the desolate place. They made camp and the Duke sent out spies to find out the whereabouts of the rest of the party under the King's command. Piers begged to go, but the Duke curtly refused him permission.

'No, Piers, these men know every inch of the country. You would only be in the way.' He turned away, his mind already occupied with more important matters and Piers began at once to help with the loading of the Duke's equipment.

They ate round the camp fire and when the squires decided that they would not be missed, for their respective masters were engaged in solemn conference, they drew away from the group and began to walk inland.

'Am I thankful to be ashore,' Guy said, with a relieved sigh.

'I'm sick of sitting about doing nothing. No one will notice, let's do some foraging.'

Piers glanced back just once at the group round the fire, then nodded, and the two ran quickly away, uphill to the shadow of some bushes.

'I wonder where we are, Piers.'

'Garth said, he thought, near Goole.'

'Well, I hope we soon meet up with the King's division.'

'And I, I'm hungry for action.'

'Oh bloodthirsty one,' laughed Guy, 'we'll soon see enough of that, I'm thinking.'

'Guy,' said Piers soberly, 'do you think the King has a chance?'

'I don't know. Warwick is an able commander and he still holds Clarence. It depends on the common people, as I see it. The King has charm, he can win them to his cause, if he has a mind to and that he must, for if he fails this time . . . ' Guy's voice trailed off and Piers flung himself down on the heather and idly pulled at the flowering clumps.

'I think Gloucester hates the thought of fighting his own brother and Warwick, who brought him up.' Piers did not mention the Lady Anne, who in his opinion figured as the main reason why Gloucester had no desire to orphan her or widow her sister.

'Guy, if we climbed that tree, we would have a good view of all this part of the country. We shall need to know our nearest farmhouse, when we are looking for food tomorrow.'

'Right, up you go.'

Both lads were able climbers and by cautiously testing footholds, they were soon ensconced in the highest part of the tree, with little harm to their persons, but slightly grazed knees and hands. From that lofty perch, they could see the country for miles around.

'That cart track must join the York Road,' said Piers, as he pointed to a narrow ribbon of roadway winding its way across the moorland. To the south-east the River Ouse swept on towards the sea.

'Aye, that's it right enough, but look Piers, over there, on the shore, no to the north, can you see, small spirals of smoke?'

'Yes, I believe I can. It's a big fire to be seen from this distance.'

'It's right on shore. Could it be a ship?'

'A ship,' Piers clutched his arm and the two turned and looked at one another in sudden doubt.

'No, it couldn't be,' Guy whispered.

'Who else would burn a ship? If the King's landing were discovered, what more likely than that they would be attacked and the ships destroyed?'

'It might be a small house or tavern on the harbour front.'

'It might and it might not,' Piers said grimly, 'but I say it's wiser to take no chances. Come on. I'm going down.'

They descended the tree in some haste and sped swiftly back to camp. When the lads arrived, the men were busy unloading gear and erecting tents for the night. Sentries had already been posted, for the Duke had no intention of being taken by a surprise attack. The boys looked around for someone in authority, and at last their gaze fell on Jehan Treves, who was ordering the disposal of supplies.

Both boys respected the sturdy soldier who had taught them how to bear their arms. He had been among the small group of loyal gentlemen and servants who had accompanied the King ot his enforced exile.

'We've seen something, Jehan,' Piers announced breathlessly.

'I've no doubt you did. You usually do,' Jehan said, grimly. 'What is it now?'

'Smoke,' Guy said hastily, 'about four or five miles north, on the coast.'

Jehan's head jerked up suddenly. 'You are sure it was on the coast?'

'Yes, sir.'

'We had better inform the Duke. He's in his tent.'

The three of them moved over to Gloucester's tent, easily recognisable by the device of the white boar on the banner floating before it. The sentry saluted as Piers swept aside the flap and requested permission to enter. The Duke was obviously engaged in planning his campaign. He looked up at Piers's voice and nodded briefly. Jehan entered first and came to stiff attention in front of the improvised table. The Duke frowned. 'Nothing wrong, I hope,' he said quietly.

'Not with the arrangements, Your Grace, but,' Jehan turned and indicated the boys in the background, 'I think these two boys may have news of the King.'

'News of the King?' The Duke turned impatiently to Piers. 'What is this, lad? Speak quickly.'

Piers repeated hurriedly what they had told Jehan. The knuckles round the quill pen, which the Duke was resting on the table, whitened suddenly. He rose clumsily to his feet. 'Strike camp, Jehan, at once.'

'But, your Grace, that smoke might mean anything.'

'It is more than likely to be what is left of the King's army and you know it, Jehan.'

'We march then, your Grace?'

'At once. About five miles north, you say. Sounds like,' he hesitated and looked over the map, 'Here.' He stabbed a finger on the small town of Holderness and looked up at the boys.

'I wouldn't say as far as that, your Grace,' Guy said quietly, 'but certainly in that direction.'

'We are about here. There's Goole over there on the river. We will march north. We may meet up with remnants of the King's army and, please God, His Grace himself. Now hurry, boys, about your business. Ask Sir Francis Lovell to come to me when he is armed. Jehan, ask the other gentlemen in the company to attend me, before we leave. Thank you, you may go.'

Jehan and Guy bowed themselves out and the Duke turned to his squire. 'Come, Piers, help me to arm. We may have wasted enough time already.'

CHAPTER ELEVEN

Gloucester was delighted to discover that his fears concerning his brother's safety were groundless. When the two armies met the reason for the smoke was explained.

'Aye, Dickon, I'm glad to see you safe,' the King said, leaning from his saddle to grip his brother's hand affectionately. He seemed to Piers more than ever to resemble some Greek God, sitting enthroned on his stallion, his face flushed with genuine delight at the thought of the coming combat. He was obviously in the highest of spirits and fully expected victory. 'You see how sure I am, gentlemen, I feel it here in my heart. I've burnt the ships, so we can't return. I either stay and conquer, or die England's King.'

'Burnt the ships, Sire, so that is what my squire saw and what brought us hurriedly in this direction,' said the Duke, as he rode by his brother's side at the head of the column, 'but if I saw it, so have others.'

'Aye, and I'm not sorry. It is time Warwick knew Edward Plantagenet is a man to be reckoned with. We ride on to York to demand entrance to the city. Truly, Dickon, I believe boldness to be the best policy. Shall the King show his own country of Yorkshire that he is afraid to face the Kingmaker?'

Gloucester smiled in answer. 'Only be discreet, Sire. It is your welfare that most concerns us, your loyal subjects.'

The King's high hopes were destined to be fulfilled. The small army was soon swelled by loyal yeoman-stock who flocked to the Yorkist cause. York opened her gates and the King and his party were welcomed, the army provisioned and billeted, but Edward was anxious to proceed to London. He knew that Queen Margaret and the young Prince Edward were to land soon and he had no desire for her army to join forces with Warwick's. He planned to fight and defeat Warwick before turning his attention to the Queen.

His army encountered no opposition. Warned by his spies, Edward was able to avoid Montecute's force at Pontefract and the great Earl of Warwick himself was encamped at Coventry. Edward demanded the city gates should be opened to him and received no reply. The Earl refused to fight when challenged, obviously he was waiting for a relief force with Queen Margaret. Edward, disgusted, determined to continue the march on London. Near Banbury, they were warned of the approach of Clarence. The King immediately called a halt and the army encamped about three miles outside the town.

Piers stood watching as the men hurried to erect the tent. Guy sauntered over and threw himself lightly down on the grass.

'This is it then,' he said, with a faint shrug, 'your first taste of action, my lad. Clarence stands between us and London and the King will fight, indeed he must fight.'

'It is strange we have not had to fight before this.'

'The King was ever lucky.' Guy shivered slightly. 'The wind is getting up. It will be a blustery night, I'm thinking. Well, if we must fight, I hope we soon do and get it over. Then we can return to London.'

Supper over, the whole party repaired to the tents to catch as much rest as they could, for all feared the commencement of the battle, the next day. The Duke of Gloucester came in quite early. Piers was surprised, for often, on the march, the young Duke had stayed with the King, discussing arrangements, until the early hours of the morning. He limped into the tent and Piers hurried over to assist him disrobe. To Piers, he seemed more than usually morose, thanking the boy but curtly for his services. For a while, he rested moodily, playing with the hilt of his dagger. Piers curled himself up in a sleeping blanket close to the camp fire outside and the rhythmic beat of the watchful sentry's feet. Lulled by these sounds, he was soon fast asleep.

Just what awakened him he never knew. One moment he was sleeping peacefully, wrapped in his blanket, and the next he was sitting up, suddenly wide awake, his eyes peering round the gloom of the tent. He strained his ears to catch the sound which must have startled him into wakefulness, but there was nothing. Outside, it was perfectly still. The fire seemed to have died down and there was no sound of the sentry's feet. Momentarily he must have moved away from the tent.

Quietly, Piers pushed aside the blanket and stood up. It took him only a moment to realise that, apart from himself, the tent was empty. The Duke of Gloucester had left. The pile of blankets lay, somewhat crumpled, where he had been resting, but of the Duke himself there was no sign. Piers dashed aside the tent flap and went out into the clearing. All was quiet. In the distance the guard stood watchful, bow slung over his shoulder. Piers stared around. Somehow, he must inform the guard of the Duke's disappearance.

He called softly, 'Hallo, over here, to me.' Startled, the bowman swung round and at the same instant Piers felt a hand pressed over his mouth, and steely arms forcing his own down by his side.

'Quiet, do you want to awaken the whole camp? Go back into the tent.'

Piers stood amazed, but obedience was strong within him, and he did as he was bidden. He heard the Duke's soft whisper to the guard.

'All is well, sirrah. It is I, Gloucester. The boy was startled, that is all. I may ride for a while in the moonlight. Return to your post and keep silent,' then he stooped and entered the tent. 'Now attend to me, Piers. I wish you to stay here and go back to sleep at once.'

Piers's eyes widened with astonishment, for the Duke was booted and spurred as if for a journey. 'But, my lord . . . ' he whispered.

The grey eyes flashed angrily. 'Do you dare bandy words with me? Do as you are bidden. As I told the guard, I intend to ride for a while.'

'Alone, my lord?'

'Alone.'

'May I not go with you?' Piers ventured.

'You may not,' was the grim answer. He looked sternly back at the boy just once more, his hand on the tent flap. 'Remember, I expect you to obey me.'

Piers flushed, lowered his head and the Duke was gone out into the night. He heard a whispered word of command, muffled hoofbeats and then silence. He stood irresolute in the shadows of the tent, one thought uppermost in his mind. His master was going into danger – and alone. Why the Duke of Gloucester should be stealing off secretly in the dead of night, while the army was camped within three short miles of the enemy, was incomprehensible to Piers. Not for a moment did he doubt the Duke's intentions. Many a man might have had the gravest doubts concerning the Duke's loyalty, but not Piers. He knew that the Duke had gone to spy out the lie of the land for his brother, the King. He knew, without trying, that he would be unable to sleep. How was he to pass the next few hours? On no account was he to divulge the truth of the Duke's absence to the rest of the camp, but suppose he was hurt or captured? No one would know what had happened or where he was held. Now if his squire had been with him in such an eventuality, he could ride back and fetch help, should it be needed.

Piers hesitated no longer. He sprang up and once more crept out of the tent. It was icy cold and the wind was getting up. The Duke would have a wild ride. If the wind dropped later, there would be rain. He reckoned that the time was getting on for about one o'clock. The sentry had moved away behind the King's tent. There were four of them altogether on duty. They were probably stealing a few moments to gossip somewhere out of the icy wind. One could hardly blame them, Piers thought. He wrapped himself up warmly in his cloak and slipped up his hood, concealing his clothing and badges of service and crept quietly towards the horses.

As he had guessed, there was no one guarding them. Obviously he had been right. They were having a quiet discussion somewhere. Since this suited his purpose, he had little cause to grumble. He chose his own horse, a frisky chestnut, and quietened it with a soft whisper. Once again, he thanked his stars that he had a way with horses. It was the work of but a few moments to harness him and be up in the saddle. Trotting the horse on the grass, so as to muffle the sound of his departure, he cantered swiftly away.

Instinctively, he took the road to Banbury. Gloucester's destination, he was sure, was the Duke of Clarence's camp. It was a cold ride but he soon got his circulation going, for he rode hard to get as near to his master in as short a time as possible. The road was clear straight before him and he had no fear of missing his way.

Half an hour later he drew rein and patted the satiny coat of his mount warningly. He was very near to the camp now. He could see the tents with their waving banners quite clearly in the moonlight. He was on enemy ground. He knew that, should he be caught, he would be hanged as a spy, so from now on he must use the utmost caution. He decided it would be easier to reconnoitre on foot, so he dismounted and made fast his horse to an overhanging bough, then moved quietly forward.

The camp was much the same as the King's. He soon perceived two guards moving quickly about blowing on their hands to try and get a little warmth into them. Everything was quiet and there was no sign of the Duke. The camp was quite large. Clarence had a considerable force at his disposal. It promised to be quite a battle in the morning, Piers thought, if he should be back to see it. Not for the first time, he wondered about the outcome. If the King should lose . . . He shivered and pushed the thought resolutely to the back of his mind.

He circled the camp, keeping close within the shadows, well out of range of the watchful sentries. Where could Gloucester be? Could he have been taken captive already? If so, he felt, the camp would be considerably more awake than it was. The capture of one of the enemy commanders would surely have called forth more activity than this. Could he have been mistaken? Had the Duke merely ridden out because he had been unable to sleep and to calm his mind before the morning? If so, he had risked his furious anger for nothing and he had better return before further harm was done. He waited for a few minutes, his eyes searching the encampment, taking in any details that might prove beneficial to the King's cause, then made his way, as silently as he had come, to where his horse stood waiting. He touched the animal's nose gently, then bent to undo the rein. Before he could lift his head, he felt cold steel pressed against the back of his neck.

'Stand still, or I won't answer for the consequences.'

He obeyed, for there was a world of menace in the voice. He felt a hand reach out and take the dagger from his sheath and then search his clothing for other weapons.

'Now straighten up and turn towards me, but don't try to jump me, for I am well known for my skill with my poniard and I should hate to send you to face your Maker without even a brief confession on your lips.'

A faint frown creased Piers's brow, even as he stood with his back to his assailant, for the voice was distinctly familiar. He turned slowly, as he was commanded, and looked into the cold, purposeful eyes of Charles Beaumont. The other gave a faint start of surprise, then the scornful lips curved into a grim smile.

'The Stable Knight! I might have known by the smell of the stables. No – keep back,' for Piers had moved forward, involuntarily angry colour flooding his cheeks. 'Now what should you be doing here at this hour of the night? No answer? Does Gloucester use his squires as spies now?' Again he smiled, as Piers stood silent. 'What can one expect when a groom is suddenly elevated to a squire's position? It is hardly to be expected that he would act honestly, like a man of breeding. No one but a base-born fool would creep here in the middle of the night to spy upon the enemy.'

'If you spoke like that to me when we were both armed,' Piers said softly, but with fury in his whispered words, 'you would not now be standing to utter any other speeches.'

'But we are not both armed, Master Spy,' the other lightly mocked, 'nor is there likely to be an occasion when we shall be, for once you are brought before the Duke of Clarence on a charge of spying, I shouldn't imagine there will be much time wasted before you are dangling from the nearest convenient tree. Now move in front of me and don't try any tricks.'

Piers lifted his shoulders in a sudden philosophical shrug. He had cast the die and lost. He had far more sense than to try and rush the other, for he knew Charles Beaumont was no mean opponent and it was possible that his death might not be so imminent as the other supposed. If it were indeed delayed until after the morning's battle, who could foretell what might happen? For the present, he was content to allow events to take their course. In spite of this, he felt a sense of deep shame at being such a fool to fall into the trap. He moved woslly, at the other's prompting, into the circle of the encampment.

'Guard, hallo there.'

Almost instantly, a burly, middle-aged archer appeared and stood to attention. Beaumont indicated Piers with a disdainful wave of his hand. 'I find a spy here in our own encampment. Bind this fellow's wrists, tightly now.'

Piers stared down at his pinioned wrists and tried to stem the tide of panic welling up within him. There was little hope of escape now. At any moment the Duke of Clarence would give the order for him to be hanged. At any rate, he conjectured, it was said to be a quick death – unless – he shivered suddenly as it occurred to him that the Duke of Clarence might not be so anxious to dispatch him in a hurry. He had come from the King's camp. He had valuable information concerning the number and armoury of the enemy. It might be that he would be pressed to divulge that information. Piers was not at all certain that he would be brave enough to endure if sufficient pressure was exerted.

Between two guards he was marched to the entrance of Clarence's tent. Charles Beaumont pushed back the flap and motioned for the guards to take Piers within. One of them pushed him roughly and he stumbled into the richly caparisoned apartment. The tent was lighted by hanging lamps and the sudden change from darkness to light momentarily dazzled him. Two figures were seated at the extreme end on stools. One of the men rose and came forward into the direct glare of the lamp. He was frowning at the interruption. It was the Duke of Clarence, the King's brother.

'Charles, how dare you burst in on me so unceremoniously?' he thundered angrily. 'I am in consultation and concerned with a matter that will brook no delay. Dismiss these guards at once.' His eyes flickered over Piers's dishevelled figure and pinioned wrists. 'What is this? What is he doing here in my tent?'

Charles Beaumont did not appear to be in the least disturbed by his master's evident displeasure. Completely confident, he indicated Piers with a disdainful movement of his hand. 'I found this creature of Gloucester's crawling about the camp. He was making an estimation of our force and supplies. I decided you would want to deal with him swiftly.'

Piers noticed, faintly surprised, that the Duke coloured hurriedly, as though in doubt about something. He bit his lip in perplexity, while his squire raised his eyebrows, surprised at his indecision. Behind the Duke of Clarence, the other man rose and entered the glow of the lamp. The light glimmered on his slight, familiar figure. Piers rocked on his feet in astonishment. The Duke of Gloucester was smiling calmly, although it was evident by the cold glitter in his grey eyes that he was angry.

'I'm sorry, George,' he said, 'that this should happen to disturb our conference. My squire suffers from a sense of overdeveloped zeal. He was ordered to remain behind in my tent.'

'Release him,' Clarence ordered, shortly.

Charles looked once at his master, then drew his dagger, crossed to Piers and severed his bonds. Feelingly, Piers massaged his numbed wrists, his eyes downcast. Well he knew that expression in his master's eyes. He deemed it wiser to say nothing. In spite of everything, he could not prevent a slight grin forming, as he stole a glance at Beaumont's furiously angry young face.

'Well, George, am I to have my answer?' Gloucester's voice, cool and steady, cut into his thoughts. 'Do you come with me tonight, or not?'

Again Clarence bit his lip and for a moment turned his back on his younger brother. 'I don't find this easy, Dickon,' he said hesitatingly, 'Warwick is my father-in-law.'

'Do you think I find it easy to come to you and beg you to return to your allegiance?' For the first time there was a note of anger in Richard's voice. 'For our mother's sake, I would not have us fight each other. Come with me, make your peace with Edward and there will be no battle in the morning, for I warn you, George, if you refuse now, Edward will have no mercy after you are defeated.'

'Are you so sure of victory?'

'I am quite sure of victory,' Richard replied quietly. The other shrugged then smiled. He was like the King, Piers thought, handsome and charming, but there was weakness in the line of the jaw and greed in the set of the lips. George of Clarence was not a man to be trusted. 'Very well, Dickon, if you wish it, for our mother's sake, I will come with you.'

Piers saw a shadow cross his master's face. Was it relief or doubt? He held out his hand and gracefully Clarence grasped it.

'To our new-found friendship, brother. You shall drink with me.' Gravely Richard nodded and Clarence swung round to face Charles Beaumont. 'Wine, Charles, for my brother Gloucester and I.' Beaumont bowed and left the tent. He returned a few moments later with two goblets and a wine bottle. Clarence poured out, then lifted his own smilingly. 'To the King and the White Rose of York,' he said as he drained it. The Duke followed his example and said simply, 'The King.'

In the early hours of the morning, Clarence rode with his brother Gloucester to the King's camp, where he was received and welcomed. Gracefully, he begged his brother's pardon and the two clasped hands in friendship. Edward was delighted. Richard limped away to his tent. He had succeeded. The two men he cared for most were reunited. There would be no battle between the brothers. Silently, Piers packed the Duke's equipment ready for the journey. The King's army now prepared to advance towards London where the Queen awaited and the son he had not yet seen, England's heir.

CHAPTER TWELVE

Flushed with pleasure, Piers rode into the yard of the Golden Cockerel. Bess flew out to greet him.

'Master Piers, the good Lord be praised, you've come back to us.' Her good-natured face shone with happiness and she shepherded him through the tap-room into the private parlour at the back. 'Here, let me look at you. You've grown.'

'Tush, Bess, I've altered little.'

'Ah, that you have. You speak and act differently. His Grace of Gloucester's trusted squire you are, that's a position to be proud of.'

Jake Garnet strode into the chamber, his huge hand eagerly out to greet his visitor. 'God bless you lad. 'Tis glad we are to see you back. Sit ye down.'

'Is business good?' Piers asked as Jake sank down on the settle beside him.

'Aye, good enough, but I could wish the country more settled, lad.'

'There'll be fighting,' Piers said quietly.

'Aye lad, in plenty.'

Later the three of them sat down to a hearty meal and Piers judged it convenient to broach a subject near to his heart. 'Have you news of Mistress Standish?'

They looked at one another, then back at Piers. Not a word was spoken, yet Piers was vaguely disturbed. 'There is nothing wrong?'

'No, lad,' Jake said hastily, 'nothing. Mistress Standish is in good health. She serves the Lady Anne as ever, but we wondered if you had heard the news. She is betrothed.'

'Betrothed?' Piers heard himself whisper the word, wonderingly, 'betrothed to whom?'

'Why to Master Charles Beaumont. They are to be wed, when he wins his spurs,' Jake said quietly.

'No,' Piers turned abruptly away. 'Is she . . . I mean . . . does she love him?'

'Why, Master Piers,' Bess said, laughingly, ''tis not a matter of love. The Duke of Clarence wishes the match and the Earl of Warwick consented. Master Charles comes from a great family. Mistress Alicia is an heiress and brings him wealth. He will make her a countess. 'Tis a good arrangement.'

'Yes, I see,' Piers smiled faintly. 'I had not thought of it in that way. Alicia seemed so young. It had not occurred to me that she would be yet contracted in marriage.'

'She is past fourteen,' Bess said, 'many noble ladies are wed by then.'

Piers nodded without speaking, then lowered his head once more and gave his attention to the food before him. When at last he rose to go, he said, 'It is a comfort to know I have friends in Chepeside.'

'Aye, lad,' Jake said. 'That you have. We're here if ever you need us.' He walked with Piers to the door and stood with him while the groom saddled his horse. 'Be wary in battle,' he said gravely.

Bess pushed past her father. There were tears in her eyes. She whispered awkwardly, 'God go with you, Piers, and bring you safely back to your friends.' She thrust something hastily into his hand and then turned and dashed back into the inn. It was a small silver Christopher medallion, on one side of which was embossed a likeness of the Virgin and Child. He looked up at the innkeeper and silently held out his hand. Jake gripped it hard, then he tucked away his medallion in his doublet for safe keeping and mounted his horse. A moment later, he was once more out in the London streets.

On the Saturday before Easter day, the news for which all had waited came. Warwick had left Coventry and was marching on London. Swiftly the King gathered his forces and marched to meet him. The two armies met just outside Barnet.

Piers would never forget that nightmare journey. There had been heavy rain and the roads and fields were slippery with mud. It was dark and he rode blindly on, relying on the man in front to show the way. The horses slipped on the greasy road surfaces and he could hear the curses of the men, as they trudged on.

Piers sat with Guy outside the tent, giving the armour and

weapons a last polish. Inside, they could hear the mutter of voices, while the King gave his knights their positions in the battle array. From time to time, they could hear the heavy boom of Warwick's guns. Guy looked up as the little tableaux round the tent flap were suddenly illumined by a red flare. 'He's close,' he commented, briefly.

Piers sniffed the air heavy with the damp cloying mist and the acrid scent of gunpowder.

A messenger rode in with a jingle of spurs and carried his news into the King's tent.

'Are you afraid of the outcome of tomorrow's battle, Guy?' Piers asked, thoughtfully.

'I'm not looking forward to having my throat cut.'

'You think victory is doubtful?'

Guy shrugged philosophically. 'There is always an element of risk in any battle.'

The commanders were issuing from the King's tent and both boys stood up respectfully. Sir Francis Lovell bade the King 'Good night,' and strode off to his quarters, Guy following. The Duke of Gloucester walked over to his own tent and stood looking out at the encampment, his hand on the flap, then he beckoned curtly to Piers and passed inside.

Piers passed a restless night. The ground was cold and clammy, and he tossed about continually. The bitter cold made his teeth chatter and he lay wakeful, staring into the darkness of the tent. Just before morning, he fell into an uneasy doze and woke to hear men marching, the squeaking of harness and the jingle of accoutrements. He sat up hastily to find the Duke dressed but not yet armed.

'You must get up, lad, if you wish to eat today,' he said, and turned away. Piers stood up and went outside the tent. a thick fog completely enshrouded the encampment. All about him, men went about their business and some knelt openly, unashamed, to pray. He splashed cold water on his face and hands and, thus refreshed, went back to his master. He ate little, for he felt it would choke him. There was a strange rumbling in his stomach. Richard sat on a small camp-stool, writing. A prayer book lay open on the improvised desk. The Duke seemed calm enough, but his young face appeared drawn and pale. Having completed his business, he threw down the quill and rose to his feet.

' 'Tis time to arm, Piers,' he said quietly.

Piers armed him with shaking fingers. In the pallid dawn his fingers were cold and stiff and he found it difficult to deal with refractory buckles on the harness. At last, it was done and Gloucester stood armed but unhelmed, one steel gauntlet on, the other in his hand. He went outside to be greeted gravely by the King and with sardonic humour by his brother, George of Clarence. With due reverence, the King knelt bareheaded to pray, his brothers beside him. Piers fought a feeling of rising panic within him. This might well be the last time he saw his master alive.

Gloucester was to have charge of the right wing. The King, with Clarence, would take the centre. Lord Hastings was to command the left wing. The three brothers embraced and the various commands moved to take their positions. The Duke strode over to Piers, who held his horse's head. He swung himself into the saddle and smiled down at his little force. Slim and proud he sat, one hand on his hip, what pale dawn light there was touching his brown hair.

'Well, gentlemen,' he said, quietly, 'I do not have to tell you what is at stake. I ask you to fight for Edward and the White Rose of York.' There was an immediate roar of response.

'God save the King.'

'York and victory.'

'God and St. George.' Then, suddenly above the cries, 'God save His Grace of Gloucester.'

'Aye, aye, the White Boar of England.'

The pale face flushed momentarily. He raised his hand, and, standard advanced, the force moved forward. Richard beckoned Piers to his side.

'Stay with the horses and the baggage train. Keep watch, for I may require fresh horses or weapons. Now, this time, do as I command. Do not fail me.'

'Aye, my lord,' Piers said dully, then he lifted his face to his master's. 'God keep you,' he whispered.

The Duke's head jerked up and he stared at the lad, intently. His mailed fist touched Piers's hair lightly for a second.

'If ought goes wrong and I . . . die, I have provided for you, Piers,' he said briefly, his words for once uttered in a softer key, then, before the lad could reply, he had wheeled his horse and was away.

All morning, the two armies faced one another, the mist, like a cold, wet blanket, between them. By afternoon, it had cleared somewhat and the King commanded the attack. The two armies closed. Piers, by the baggage train, could distinguish little. He could hear the screams of dying horses, the shouts of the men as they charged at one another with sword and battle axe. The air was acrid with powder and there was a sickening stench of blood and smoke. Back and forth the opponents swerved. Oxford, fighting on Warwick's left, fell on Lord Hastings's force, which broke and fell back to Barnet. A sweating courier brought this news to Piers, who bent to tie up a bad thigh wound for him.

'How goes the battle?'

'Oxford has chased the King's left wing back to Barnet. It's a complete rout. Some say it's the beginning of the King's defeat, but the King holds the centre, staunchly.'

'That lad – why he fights like one possessed. Never was there a fairer general. Constantly he heartens his men with shouts of, "King Edward and York".'

How long Piers stayed by the horses he could not say. It seemed to him to be at least a century. Suddenly an archer dashed up to him.

'Hasten, lad, Gloucester requires another horse. His own is badly wounded.'

Without argument Piers prepared another mount to carry the wearied man and watched as he pulled himself into the saddle and took the bridle rein of the Duke's charger from him.

' 'Tis hell,' he commented briefly. 'You can't see a hand in front of you and confusion is spreading. It is becoming increasingly difficult to know whether ye're fighting friend or foe.' He gasped suddenly and placed a hand to his breast.

'You are wounded?' Piers queried swiftly.

' 'Tis nothing.' The man urged his horse forward but, even as he spoke, his horse reared in sudden fear and he toppled forward in the saddle. Piers dashed up to him, his face white and strained.

'I have no ... control ... ' the man whispered brokenly, 'I . . . ' Abruptly, Piers found that he was supporting a dead weight in his arms. Desperately he shouted for assistance and, with the help of a groom, lifted the injured man down to the ground. He looked round for someone to deliver the horse to the sore-beset Duke, but there was none by. He swung himself into the other saddle, took the Duke's mount by the bridle rein, and plunged forward.

The mist swirled back for a moment, as he rode into the thick of the battle, so that he was able to glimpse the carnage. Men fought hand over hand in the deep mud. Horses thrashed about in their death agonies, for there were none to put an end to their misery. Face set, he forced his way past and headed for Gloucester's standard, right in the thickest of the fighting. His horses were fresh and he managed to avoid all who sought to stay him. One knight aimed a vicious blow at him with a battleaxe. Arrows flew round his head. He could hear the whine of them and one grazed his cheek. He tasted the salt tang, where the blood trickled into his mouth, but hardly sensed the pain. At last, he was by the Duke's side.

'You messenger fell,' he panted.

Gloucester nodded as he changed mounts. 'Right, lad – now get back to the baggage train.'

Piers fell back. The Duke was hidden from his view almost at once. He pressed for his former position, but the enemy had closed round him. Now, he was forced to fight for his life. He drew his sword and used it to parry the blows of his attackers. He seemed not to feel the weariness of his arm or the pain when he was blooded. Slowly, surely, he pressed his now single opponent back, feeling the sudden savagery of confidence in his own powers. Then suddenly, disaster overtook him.

Towards him, mounted on a superb grey, charged one of Montecute's knights. In that one second, Piers noted the battle-axe poised in his mailed fist. Piers's horse whinnied, shrill with terror, and reared. Desperately Piers fought for control of his mount and in that moment the other struck. He felt white-hot pain in his shoulder and screamed aloud with the agony. A feeling of deadly sickness engulfed him and his sword fell nerveless from his hand. Blindly he sought to regain his seat, but the agony in his shoulder was unbearable. He fell from the saddle and only narrowly missed being trampled to death by the hoofs of his fear-maddened horse. Swiftly, he stumbled to his knees and with his uninjured hand drew his dagger. A red mist swam before his eyes. The pain was unbearable. He forced himself to retain his senses, as he could just discern four archers swoop down upon him. This is it, he thought briefly, and so great was the agony of his wound that he was past caring. He slipped forward on to his knees as he tried to rise, then suddenly there was a silence. A voice called something indistinguishable to the fainting youth. He was conscious of someone standing over him, protecting him with his body, a familiar form with bronze hair wet with the mist . . . and then the redness before his eyes deepened and deepened into blackness and Piers toppled forward and knew no more.

*   *   *

'Would the fog never go,' Piers wondered, as he moved slightly, shaking his head from side to side to clear his vision. Articles and forms began to take shape, and he found himself lying on a pallet. Wonderingly, he gazed round, taking in the familiar stools and equipment of Gloucester's tent. There was a stiffness in his limbs as he tried to move them and his head ached. His searching fingers touched something soft and warm and, lifting himself painfully, he saw that the Duke's velvet cloak had been placed under him. The movement, slight as it was, brought a sharp, agonising sensation to his shoulder, as though it were being pierced by red-hot needles and he gasped with the suddenness of the pain.

At the sound, a slight figure over the other side of the tent jerked round and hurried across to the pallet.

'Piers – you are conscious,' Guy Tremaine said, his young face strained and pale with anxiety.

Piers sank back, wearied with the effort of moving. Guy knelt beside him and, lifting his head, tucked another cloak, which had formed a rough pillow, more comfortably beneath his head.

'Lie still, Piers. The physician says you must rest. You have lost a deal of blood. You are safe. You're back in the tent.'

'How did I get here?' Piers whispered hoarsely.

'Two archers brought you, on a bier.'

'How goes the battle?'

' 'Tis over. The King is victorious; there is naught to fear.'

'And Gloucester?' Once more Piers tried to sit up and was gently pushed back by his friend.

'Quite safe. He's out with the King at the moment. He left me here to look after you.'

A little sigh escaped Piers's lips and he fell back on the pallet and was silent, while Guy gazed down at him anxiously.

'He saved my life, Guy,' he said at last, 'dismounted and

stood over me. That's all I can remember, seeing him there . . . then I must have fainted.'

'Yes, all right, but you must be still and keep quiet.'

'First tell me about the battle.'

'If you promise to remain quiet.'

Piers smiled meekly, 'I promise.'

Guy fetched over one of the camp stools and seated himself by the improvised couch.

'Very well, you heard that Oxford chased Lord Hastings's men as far as Barnet?' Piers nodded. 'Good. Then Oxford ordered them to return and attack the King's flank. Instead of that, they mistook their direction in the fog and came up behind their own. What happened no one knows, but 'tis thought that Warwick's men thought the star emblazoned on the livery of Oxford's retainers to be the King's device – the sun in splendour – and they began to fight each other. That about ended it for Warwick. Gloucester's wing swept though his left flank and there was a complete rout of his army.'

'Is the Kingmaker taken?'

'He was killed with his brother, Montecute.'

Piers crossed himself devoutly. 'God rest his soul. Never was there a braver knight.'

Before Guy could answer, the Duke of Gloucester strode into the tent. Seeing Piers conscious, he limped over to him, while Guy respectfully drew back.

'How are you feeling, Piers?' he enquired.

'Better, my lord.'

Gloucester smiled grimly down at him. 'You lost a deal of blood, but the sawbones says your wound will heal within a day or two. You were lucky. A blow like that might have crushed your shoulder.'

He drew off his gauntlet and motioned to Guy. 'Bring me some wine, Guy.'

When the squire brought it, he stooped, and lifting Piers's head, assisted him to drink. As he sank back on the pillow, the Duke smoothed back his sweat-dampened chestnut hair with a cool hand. The boy's face was flushed and he touched the hot forehead thoughtfully.

'We won,' Piers whispered.

'Yes, now be quiet. I'm going to leave you to rest.'

'My lord,' the soft whisper arrested the Duke as he made to leave the tent.

'Well?' he queried curtly.

'You risked your life for me. Why'

'It was foolish. I might have endangered the King's cause'.

'Why did you do it?'

Richard smiled a little grimly. 'To tell the truth, I believe it was idleness.'

'Idleness?'

'I never could take the trouble to train another squire when once I'd got used to one.'

Piers looked up at him puzzled, until without another word he left the tent.

CHAPTER THIRTEEN

Wearied beyond thought, Piers stood at the tent flap and heard the water splash into the bowl. He could hear the Duke speaking to the surgeon who was dressing his wound.

'You say I am not to use this arm for a while?'

'No, my lord. I advise you to have it in a sling for a week or so and give the muscle time to repair itself.'

'Aye, if there is no more fighting. Thank you, master surgeon, you can go. I shall be well enough now.'

Piers turned into the tent as the physician bowed respectfully and withdrew. The Duke beckoned him forward.

'Did you hear him?'

'I did, sir.'

'A similar wound to yours. It has cut through the muscle. It would have to happen just now. Can you clear away that mess, lad?' Piers was about to obey him when the tent flap was unceremoniously swept aside and the King followed by the Duke of Clarence strode in.

'Dickon,' the King's face showed his concern. 'How is your wound?'

Gloucester grimaced. 'Little enough to be dangerous, Sire, and great enough to inconvenience me for a while. It is naught. Will you sit down?'

Piers spoke respectfully to his master. 'Do you wish me to leave you, sir?'

The Duke looked enquiringly at his brother, who shook his head.

'Nay, lad, there's no need for you to go. Carry on with your work. They tell me he fought well, Dickon. We shall show our pleasure in a more worthy way when we return to London, Piers. In the meantime, be assured of our good will.'

Piers bowed respectfully and retired to the far side of the

tent, where the conversation of the Royal Princes could not be overheard by him.

It was over. Outside Tewkesbury, the King had finally defeated Margaret of Anjou and was safely established on his throne. For weeks, they had done naught but march wearily over muddy fields and sleep in tents. Such a short time they had spent in London after the King returned victorious from Barnet, barely time for Gloucester to assure his mother of his safety, and even less time for a reverent burial of the Earl of Warwick, before the King's army was once more on the move, this time on the heels of Queen Margaret, who with Edward, the Prince of Wales, the betrothed of the Lady Anne Neville, had landed at Southampton, only to learn of Warwick's defeat and death.

The Queen had been anxious to return to France but, heartened by her supporters, had decided to stay and face the King's army. The die was cast at Tewkesbury. The Queen lost everything. Her commanders were slain and Edward, the delight of her heart, younger by a year than the Duke of Gloucester, was slain in his first battle.

Richard of Gloucester had command of the van and had pressed the attack. Piers could feel now that scrambling advance over the rough ground, floundering into ditches, the noise, the stench, the dirt and uproar of the battle. Gloucester fought like one possessed. Again and again, he charged into the foremost of the enemy, brandishing his sword and heartening his men by his daring. It was in the battle that he had got the wound in his arm the surgeon had just been dressing. Two battles in so short a time, and so many good Englishmen slain. Now, at last, Piers thought, it may be possible for there to be peace in England.

He passed a hand over his eyes to dispel the sudden horror of the sounds and sights he had witnessed; of the young Prince, crushed to death by the retreating horsemen, his golden hair all dappled with blood, of the enemy knights slain by the orders of the King and the noise and confusion of the rout, horses dying, men screaming with fear. He shuddered and bent to his tasks with greater diligence, seeking for something which would, for a short while, banish the horror of the combat from his mind.

The King and the Duke of Clarence rose to their feet. The short conference had come to an end.

'I may ride to Gupshill then?' Piers noticed that the Duke's question carried a note of unusual urgency. The Duke of Clarence interrupted hastily.

'I would not deem it wise for Dickon to ride to Gupshill or elsewhere, until he has rested his arm,' he said swiftly.

The King hesitated. 'You had better not ride just yet, Dickon,' he said.

'But I may go?' the Duke pressed, still more urgently.

'When you are fit. You should rest and besides . . . I may need you.' With this answer, he had to remain content. He swallowed his disappointment and bowed his head as the King and Clarence left the tent. He sat back on the stool, his fingers beating a sharp tattoo on the table in front of him.

'Piers,' he said at last, 'come here to me, leave whatever you are doing.'

Piers put down the breastplate with which he was engaged and crossed to his master's side. Richard looked at him keenly. 'Prepare yourself for riding. I wish you to take a message for me to Gupshill.'

Piers swung round at these words, his lips parting in the suddenness of his delight, Gupshill, the religious house where Queen Margaret had sought sanctuary with Warwick's younger daughter Anne Neville, the betrothed of the dead Prince of Wales. Piers's heart rejoiced. Where Anne Neville was, it was more than likely that there Alicia Standish would be also. Swiftly, he pulled on riding boots and armed himself.

The Duke sealed the missive and held it out to him. 'I think you know to whom this is addressed.'

'Aye, my lord.'

'You swear you will give this into the hand of the Lady Anne and none other. Tell, her . . . ' he hesitated for a moment, 'tell her, whatever happens, she is to remain with the nuns until I come to her. You understand?'

'Perfectly, sir.'

For a moment the Duke was silent, then he looked up directly into the eyes of his squire. 'You know what this means to me. You know that I dearly love the Lady Anne and she . . . she does me the honour to return my love. The King has at last given his consent to our marriage. I wish her to know of it at once. Tell her not to fear. There is naught now to prevent our marriage, and I will see to it that both she and her mother are treated fairly by the King.' He gave a little sigh and grimaced with pain. 'I wish I could ride myself, but that is impossible at the moment.'

A groom brought up Piers's horse and eyed him with marked deference. Guy came over, his eyebrows rising at the sight of Piers booted and spurred for a journey.

'I ride on Gloucester's business.'

'How is his wound?'

'Not dangerous, but painful, I suspect. Assist him if he should require help.'

'Piers, you know well enough he will let no one near him but you, but I'll gladly render him any assistance I can. Rest easy.'

Piers smiled down at his friend, then touched his mount lightly with his spurs.

For some little distance the countryside showed signs of the past encounter. The ground was trampled underfoot, crops ruined. Few men walked in the fields. The land carried an air of desolation. A little farther on, a group of archers were engaged in burying some of the dead. They saluted him as he rode by.

Once away from Tewkesbury, the countryside acquired a more pleasant aspect. Piers could see the ploughboys busy in the fields and a pedlar patiently trudging along with his heavy pack. He called to him in passing. It was a pleasant spring day and he hummed to himself as he rode. The air was fresh and clean and he could feel the weariness dropping from him, like a discarded mantle. Refreshed, he leaned forward in the saddle and whispered to his horse to carry him faster. He was riding towards Alicia and he must know how she fared. His brow clouded as he considered her betrothal. Of course, he knew it had to come, but to Charles Beaumont of all people!

An hour later, he drew rein at a small inn by the roadside, dismounted and called for service. A nervous, poorly dressed woman came to the door and eyed his livery with some wonder, tinged with suspicion. Piers smiled at her warmly. 'Tell me, good woman, am I far from Gupshill?'

'Nay, young sir, 'tis not far, less than an hour's ride,' she assured him.

'Can you give me a bowl of wine and some new bread and a cheese perhaps? I am in haste, so cannot wait for you to prepare a hot dish.'

'Aye, young sir, come in. It won't take a moment.' Piers

followed her into the inn. It was a poor hostelry, but clean. The rough tables and chairs were well polished and there were fresh rushes on the floor. He sat down on a wooden bench and she placed the food before him. He nodded his thanks and began to eat heartily, for he had not stopped for refreshment before leaving the camp. The woman had obviously been reassured from her earlier doubts concerning his character by his courteous treatment of her and she glanced at him curiously.

'Are you a messenger from the battle?'

'Yes. The King is victorious, good wife, if that is what you wish to know.'

She nodded with an odd birdlike gesture. 'Aye, I know. One came to the inn about an hour ago. He told us.'

Her words arrested Piers in the action of drinking. He lowered his tankard to the table and looked at her, thoughtfully. 'A messenger, riding this way? Where was he going?'

'He did not say, young sir, but he was in haste. About your age he would be, or a little older. Brave yellow hair he had, fair enough for a woman.'

Piers sat quiet still, one lip clenched under his teeth, while the woman chattered on. There was only one person he knew with brave yellow hair, like a woman's. He rose and went to the door.

'You are going?' She eyed him wonderingly.

'Yes, good wife, as I said, I am in haste.' He threw her a silver piece. 'This will pay for my meal, I think.'

'Indeed, sir, 'tis more than enough.'

'Good. Keep what is left. I must be off. He mounted swiftly and the woman pointed out the right road to him. He called down his thanks and once more took the road. He no longer whistled. His mind was occupied with the woman's words. Why should Charles Beaumont ride on ahead of him to the convent?

Gupshill wore an air of quiet peace and rest, as though it did not have within its walls a distraught mother and a stricken girl. Piers doffed his hat to the portress and spoke to her, courteously.

'I come from Tewkesbury, sister, and would have speech with the Lady Anne Neville.'

She opened the door and beckoned him in. Together, they walked slowly down the gravelled walk to the house. Her manner was gentle and grave, her hands devoutly clasped, her eyes cast down. He bowed his head, respectfully, when she showed him into a small room on the ground floor.

'I will inform the Lady Anne of your presence, sir. Be kind enough to wait in here.'

She withdrew and he heard the soft swish of her habit as she walked away down the corridor. The room was pleasantly warm for there was a fire burning in the open hearth and a woman's embroidery frame stood by it. He crossed over to it and looked down at the design of flowers and leaves, half completed. He was so engrossed that he did not hear the door open, until someone addressed him from behind.

'You are a messenger from Tewkesbury, the sister portress informs me. How can I assist you, sir?'

He turned and saw a tall, graceful young woman in the doorway. She was simply attired in a dress of grey velvet, a simple white coif over her dark hair. Turning, she closed the door behind her and advanced further into the room. Suddenly, recognition dawned and she stood stock still with surprise.

'Piers?'

He stared at her. It was impossible. This tall, graceful, poised creature could never be the madcap Alicia – and yet, the hazel eyes were the same, the wide, generous mouth, now breaking into a smile of welcome.

'Well, Sir Gallant, are you still dumb?'

'I . . . I . . . Why, I couldn't believe it to be truly you. You have changed, Mistress Standish.'

'And you too, sir. Over a head taller and so broad.'

'I did not mean that you had grown,' he interrupted gravely. She smiled. 'What brings you, Piers?'

'I bring a message from Gloucester, to the Lady Anne. She is here?'

'She is with the Queen and sent me to ask if your business was urgent.'

'The Queen knows that Prince Edward is dead?' Alicia turned away and walked to the fireplace.

'Yes. A messenger rode in a short time ago. He brought the news.'

Piers was awkwardly silent. 'Well, King Edward is safe on the throne at last,' he ventured, after a few moments. 'The Yorkist cause is secure. You wanted that, Alicia?'

'Yes, I wanted that, Piers, and I'm fiercely glad, but . . . '

she lifted her hands in a helpless little gesture and let them drop again. 'If you could see the Queen. She is like one possessed, poor soul. The Prince was the light of her life. Aye, 'tis ever so, men must fight and women must weep. How are the King and Gloucester?'

'The King, well. Gloucester has a shoulder wound which prevents him temporarily from riding. That is why I am here.'

'I see.'

'The Lady Anne must feel the death of her father.'

Alicia seated herself and beckoned him to do the same, but he perched himself on the edge of the oak dining table. 'She knows not which way to turn. Her father killed, her mother in hiding and she recently betrothed to a man declared by the King to be a usurping traitor. I wonder she has not run mad. Oh Piers, when will the world be straight again, tell me?'

He smiled. 'I wish I could, Alicia, but I feel it will not be long now. Gloucester assures me none of you have aught to fear. He . . . ' He broke off as the door opened and they both rose to their feet as Anne Neville came into the room. No sorrow could mar her pale loveliness. She was dressed in black from head to foot. A golden cross caught the flickering light from the fire in the hearth, as she turned to face them.

'I have given the Queen a cooling draught and she is resting,' she said. 'Poor soul, she is distracted. She will be best alone for a while. There is no need for you to go to her.' She moved nearer to the fire, then stooped short as she caught sight of Piers, her face whitening, 'Piers Langham, what do you here?'

Piers bowed respectfully and fumbled within his doublet for the Duke's letter.

'I bring a message from My Lord of Gloucester, My Lady,' he said, and held it out to her.

To his surprise, she drew back, her eyes flashing dangerously, her breast rising and falling. At last, her voice came in a hatred-filled whisper.

'Go back, Piers – go back to that crooked devil, your master, and tell him that Anne Neville wishes never to look upon his face again.' Alicia gave an anguished little gasp and went to her mistress, but firmly, Anne put her aside.

'Why, my lady . . . ' Piers desperately searched for words to explain, completely dumbfounded by her unexpected attitude.

'My lord wishes to assure you of his love.'

'His love,' she echoed his words in a vehement little hiss, 'love he calls it. Aye, 'tis love for one person only, Richard Plantagenet. His love for me is centred on one thing, the Warwick fortune.'

'My lady, I'm sure that is not true,' Alicia interrupted breathlessly.

'Alicia, this does not concern you.' She turned away from them abruptly and, walking to the window, spoke almost to herself in a voice choked with tears.

'God knows I had every reason to wish Edward dead, but I had not thought, I . . . ' Piers saw her twist her hands tightly together in a strained, helpless gesture. 'But that Richard should kill him with his own hand. Oh no, not that. I could never face happiness when it was based on murder so foul.'

Piers stepped forward hastily. 'My lady, you surely do not believe this base lie?'

She twisted towards him, 'Tell me Edward, Prince of Wales, still lives.'

'My lady, I wish I could tell you that but I can't. The Prince was slain . . . '

'And by Richard of Gloucester.'

'Madam, the man who says that lies in his teeth.'

She pounced on his answer, 'Can you swear that is the truth? Did you, with your own eyes, see another stab the Prince?'

'No, madam, I did not, indeed, I know not who killed him, but this I do know, it was no murder. Edward was slain in fair fight on the battlefield.'

'And yet I have it, from an eye-witness, that Richard deliberately sought out the Prince and killed him.'

Piers's hand fell to his side in a gesture of weary resignation. 'If you can find it in your heart to believe that, my lady, I have nothing further to say, but since I come to deliver a message, will you not take it from my hand?'

She took the letter from him and, walking over to the fire, held it down with the tongs, until it was utterly consumed. Piers turned to see Alicia stare at him with tortured dark eyes. He shrugged helplessly and moved towards the door.

'My lady, with your permission, I will take my leave.'

'Yes, Piers.' Her voice sounded dull and lifeless. 'Go and God go with you. I do not blame you for aught that has occurred. You but serve your master.'

At the door he turned to give one last appeal. 'My lady, Gloucester begs you not to leave this house until he comes for you, for he is concerned for your safety.'

'Tell him he need concern himself no longer. I would feel more secure in a tiger's den than with Richard of Gloucester, tell him that.'

Abruptly, Piers bowed to the two ladies and left the room. He bit his lip in perplexity and started down the corridor. The meaning of Anne Neville's sudden bitterness and deadly hatred for his lord passed his simple comprehension.

'Piers,' he halted suddenly as he heard soft footsteps behind him and waited until Alicia came to a halt by his side. He stared at her dumbly, then burst out, 'Alicia, you cannot think that of him. *You* do not believe it?'

'I know not what to believe,' she faltered. 'I . . . Well Gloucester loves Anne and Edward was in his way. He . . . may have . . . '

'Do you consider that my lord lost all sense of honour?' Piers countered, hotly.

'A woman knows little about honour, Piers. She only considers love.'

'Yes, *love*,' said Piers bitterly, 'I was forgetting, you are soon to be wed. I wish you joy of it.'

She stared up at him. 'You heard, from whom?'

'I heard you were betrothed to Charles Beaumont. Jake Garnet told me.'

'We have taken no vows before the priest yet, It is not finally determined,' she said quietly.

'You care for him?'

'I do not know. We women are not consulted about these things. I was legal ward to the Earl of Warwick, who drew up this marriage settlement.'

'They tell me it is an advantageous match. He will make you a countess.'

'I suppose so.'

He stepped back and she stood quite still, her face serious, then she turned half away from him.

'I think we are neither of us in a fit state to discuss anything reasonably. I think you had better go now to Gloucester, but Piers . . . tell him, if he truly loves Anne, to risk her anger and come for her, quickly.'

101

Piers stooped to catch her by the shoulder and read the answer to her strange remark in her eyes, but she evaded him and, before he could intercept her, she had gathered up her skirts and was off along the corridor. He watched until an angle of the wall hid her from view, then shaking his head in a puzzled movement, went in search of the portress to re-open the gate for him.

CHAPTER FOURTEEN

It was Guy who greeted Piers when he rode wearily into Tewkesbury to the house that Gloucester had commandeered for his lodging. He forbore to ask questions.

'How goes it?' Piers asked quietly.

'Well enough. God grant we soon return to London.' He paused for a moment. 'Edward Beaufort was executed early this morning. He was found seeking sanctuary in Tewkesbury Abbey. The young Prince's body was borne there to await burial. Heaven help his poor mother.'

Piers sighed heavily. There were many who must suffer now that the grim fighting was over. 'Where is Gloucester?'

'Resting within his lodging. He asked that you should be taken to him the moment you arrived.'

Piers did not relish the coming interview. He was sick at heart. He turned his head, however, and rose to his feet, as he heard the Duke's familiar halting steps approach the solar.

'Rest, Piers,' he said, crossing to him and indicating the seat with a wave of his hand. 'I know you must be wearied, but I would hear your news at once. You delivered my message?'

'Aye, my lord.'

The Duke frowned slightly, sensing something was wrong. 'You saw the Lady Anne?'

'Aye, my lord.'

'She is safe and well?'

'She was safe, my lord, would I could say more.' He broke off and gazed out of the window. Gloucester's lips tightened involuntarily and he sat down opposite the boy, his hands resting lightly on the carved arms of his chair.

'Come, Piers, since when have I given you cause to be afraid of giving me bad news? What is it?' he enquired quietly.

'She would not read your letter or take heed of your message, which I gave her verbally. She bade you to keep from

103

her sight. She said she hoped never to set eyes on you again.'

'I see.'

'My lord, someone has grossly maligned you to the Lady Anne. She is convinced that you murdered Prince Edward.'

'What else did she say of me?'

'Why naught . . . my lord,' Piers faltered hastily.

'Piers?'

'I . . . she . . . she bade me return to the . . . crooked devil I served.'

The hands tightened on the carved arms of the chair so hard that the white knuckles showed out strangely in the gleam of the firelight. Piers stared up at the grim, pale face and for the space of some moments neither spoke, then the Duke said, evenly, 'You did your work well, Piers. Now, I suggest that you go to your room and rest before changing your clothing for dinner.'

Piers bowed his head and, rising moved towards the door. Suddenly, he turned. 'Charles Beaumont rode before me to Gupshill,' he said abruptly.

The Duke's eyebrows rose in surprise. 'You are sure?'

'A woman at a hostelry where I stopped to eat described him. It must have been him. My lord, he is a servant of the Duke of Clarence. I beg you not to wait, but ride now after the Lady Anne.'

'Why should you believe her to be in danger?'

Piers hesitated. It was a delicate situation and he knew not how to frame what was in his mind.

'My lord, I saw Alicia Standish at Gupshill and she warned me . . . '

'Warned you of what?'

'I . . . I do not know, Sir. Why should anyone wish to turn the heart of the Lady Anne from you, at least no one but . . . '

'But my brother Clarence, who has no desire to share the Warwick fortune with me.' Piers flushed scarlet with embarrassment, and he continued, 'I know what are his wishes. Perhaps you are right. Even if the Lady Anne will not avail herself of my protection, it would be wise if she were to stay, willingly or unwillingly, at Baynards Castle for a while. I'll ride in the morning. Now lad, off you go to rest. Make arrangements for an early start in the morning. I'll call at Gupshill, then on to London.'

104

Piers moved once more to the door, then the Duke said quietly, 'Thank you.'

He turned, and walking swiftly back to his master, his eyes alight with compassion, said. 'Sir, she did not mean it. Of that I am sure. She but spoke in the heat of the moment. Everything will work out to your advantage in the end, sir, I am convinced of it.'

'Perhaps,' Piers, perhaps,' the Duke smiled down at him sardonically, 'but we must not forget that I am indeed ill-suited to go courting a lady.'

'But under the circumstances . . . '

'I will be no party to any coercion, Piers. The Lady Anne marries me willingly or not at all.' He smiled as he said it, his eyes for once tender, then almost in the same instant, he was the same grave, sardonic young Duke. 'Now off you go. Why do I waste time bandying words with you?'

The following afternoon the royal cavalcade left for London. The King was in jocular mood. Gloucester grave and quiet, stood by his side, smiling politely when asked to share a joke, but it was evident from his expression that his thoughts were otherwise engaged. Piers knew he was impatient to be off, for the King had granted him permission to ride to Gupshill and there take into his charge Queen Margaret and the Lady Anne Neville and to bring them to London. Piers noticed that Clarence was not present. He turned to Guy, who had come down the steps from the house and was now standing behind him.

'Where's Clarence?' he asked curiously.

'I don't know,' Guy said, his eyes searching for Sir Francis Lovell among the gentlemen about the King, 'He must have ridden ahead.'

'Had he the King's permission?'

'I can't say. Why do you ask? Is it important?' He turned and looked back at Piers curiously, for there was an urgent note in his friend's tone.

'I don't know yet,' Piers said grimly, then moved forward, as he saw the little group prepare to mount at the King's signal.

During the short ride through Tewkesbury, Piers had no opportunity to speak to Gloucester, for the King kept him close by his side. He was in a fever to reach the religious house where he believed not only the Lady Anne, but Alicia too, to be in need of aid. At length, the Duke of Gloucester parted from the King, taking Sir Francis Lovell and ten men with him. This small party was to form an escort for the defeated Queen and her ladies. The moment he was on his way to the convent, Richard rode at top speed. Behind, and at a slightly more leisurely pace, came two horse-drawn litters for the captive ladies.

The portress, evincing mild surprise at the size of the party, showed them into the parlour where Piers had previously been received by the Lady Anne. The Duke limped over to the fire and stood staring down into the flames. He turned and bowed his head as a small, rather stout lady, dressed in the habit of the order, entered the room.

'You wish to see Queen Margaret, my lord – I am the Mother Superior.'

'Yes, Reverend Mother. I am sent by the King to escort Her Grace and attendant ladies to London. I am Richard of Gloucester.'

Her kindly eyes flickered over his slim figure, graceful for the moment, in repose. 'I will inform Her Grace.' At the door, she paused and turned, 'The Queen has been most upset by the news of her son's death.'

'That I can well imagine.'

'You will not take it amiss if . . . ' her voice trailed off uncertainly.

'I shall treat Her Grace with all due respect. Never fear, Reverend Mother,' he said shortly and she left them.

All turned as the door was thrown open and Margaret of Anjou entered. Piers had heard of her great beauty, which they said astonished all the court when she had first come from France to marry poor King Harry. Since then, her reputation for ruthless leadership had travelled the world. He recalled tales of her callous treatment of the Yorkists after Wakefield. He was greatly shocked at his first sight of her.

Margaret of Anjou was a broken woman. She stood stiffly still in the doorway, clad from head to foot in unrelieved mourning. Her face still bore the ravages of her unspeakable grief. Her hands shook as she clasped them and Piers had the feeling that she was only half alive. The Duke of Gloucester seemed also to be deeply shocked by her appearance, for it was some moments before he could bring himself to speak to her.

'Madam,' he said at last, his voice harsh with embarrassment, 'King Edward has sent me to escort you and your ladies to London. Are you ready to accompany me?'

'If it is the King's command,' she said dully.

'You may be assured, Madam, of our wish that you should be as comfortable as possible during the journey.'

'I am assured, my lord.'

'Then would you prepare yourself and please inform the Lady Anne Neville that, by the King's command, she is to ride with us.'

For a moment, the Queen seemed to awaken from her half trance, 'I am afraid that is impossible. The Lady Anne left with her brother-in-law, Clarence, early this morning, to join her mother and sister.'

'Clarence, you say?' His voice expressed bewilderment.

'I was told so. I did not see him,' she said coldly, and Richard realised, by the deadly hatred in her voice, that she would never forgive Clarence his betrayal of her cause. She had moved towards the door and Lovell lifted his hand to open it for her. She turned and nodded to him, then she was gone. Sir Francis stared after her.

'Richard,' he said, switching hurriedly round to face the Duke, 'why ever should the Lady Anne do that? The King gave you permission to bring her to London. Has Clarence removed her from this house in spite of the King's commands?'

The Duke did not answer him. He was staring straight in front of him, a hard set line to his young lips. At length, he turned and seemed to start from his reverie.

'Sir Franics,' he said evenly, 'will you see the Mother Superior, and give her this money, our offering towards the upkeep of this house. Guy, oversee the disposal of the Queen's baggage.'

'Sir Francis,' he said evenly, 'will you see the Mother to Guy and together, they left the room.

'Piers, attend to the litters. See that they are quite ready for the Queen. I wish to leave the moment she is ready.'

'Yes, my lord.' He turned back to stare into the fire and Piers hurried about his duties. As he stepped into the hall before the main door, where the litters were drawn up, he was arrested by a sound above him. Glancing up hastily, he saw a slight figure on the gallery above. It was a young girl dressed in the simple, white habit of a novice.

'Hist, you, young sir,' she whispered, leaning down to speak to him, 'you are in the service of the Duke of Gloucester? Know ye one, Piers Langham?'

'Yes, my little sister, I am Piers Langham. What do you want with me?'

She drew back a little and looked hurriedly around her, cautioning him to silence by a finger placed lightly on her lip.

'Stay where you are. I will come down to you.'

She vanished from the rail and he stood perplexed. A moment later, he heard the rustle of her white robe down the corridor and she was by his side.

'I cannot stop,' she whispered, 'it is forbidden for us novices to converse with strange men, but I have a package for you. I was told you would know the sender.' From the voluminous folds of her habit, she drew a small sealed package and gave it into his hands. Looking down at it, in the dim shade of the hall, he was able to recognise the hand of Alicia Standish.

'Thank you with all my heart, little sister,' he said fervently, 'you have rendered her who gave you this and one other a great service.'

'Then that is enough,' she said smiling shyly, 'now, good sir, I must return to my work in the infirmary. God speed you.'

'A blessing on you,' he murmured hurriedly, then, as she heard the sound of voices on the gallery above, she ran quickly off down the corridor. He thrust the small package out of sight in his doublet, and went outside to stand by the horses. He was in a fever of excitement to find out what Alicia had written to him, but there was no time to read her message now, for Queen Margaret and her two ladies were emerging from the house. Behind limped the Duke of Gloucester, Guy, carrying some of the bundles, and Sir Francis Lovell.

Gloucester glanced briefly at the men-at-arms, drawn up before the door, then asked the Queen if she were ready to depart. She answered in a monosyllable, then, drawing aside her skirts, as if the very proximity of his garments would contaminate them, moved disdainfully towards the first of the litters. Gloucester gestured to Sir Francis, who stepped forward and assisted her to seat herself. The two ladies got into the second litter. The baggage was then strapped on to the pack mules and the party mounted and took the road to London.

Gloucester conveyed the defeated Queen to the Tower, where she was at once taken to the apartments of her husband, poor sickly King Harry. Common gossip had it that the weak, feeble King had not long to live, the shock of the rebellion and subsequent battles having proved too much for him. He was sick in mind and body and lay not recognising those who visited and spoke with him.

The King rejoiced at Westminster with his wife, daughters and baby son. Nothing could quench his spirits now that the troubles were over and he was free to enjoy himself once again in his own lazy, self-indulgent fashion. Gloucester, deeming it wiser to wait until the morning before requesting an audience of his feckless elder brother, rode with all speed to Baynards Castle to greet his mother. Piers stabled his horse and hurried into the Great Hall where he strode over to a great burning brand, stood beneath it, and taking out Alicia's note, tore it open and read the hastily scrawled contents.

'Piers,' it read, 'the Duke of Clarence is here now and intends to take the Lady Anne with him. Our destination, I believe, is first, Beaulieu, to join the lady Isobel and the Countess of Warwick then to Clarence's own town house in London – or so he has told us. Anne has agreed to accompany him but, for reasons which I dare not state, I consider her unwise. I would talk with you further. If you can, meet me at the Golden Cockerel on Thursday afternoon. I will try to come to you then. Yours, in haste, Alicia.'

Piers sighed and thrust the letter into his doublet, then went in search of Gloucester. 'Sir,' Piers said, 'I have received a letter from Lady Alicia Standish.' A gleam of interest brightened the Duke's eyes. Piers held out to him the letter and turning towards the oil lamp, he perused its contents. Piers watched him silently. Slowly he folded the note and gave it back into Piers's hands, his face expressionless.

'For once, you have seen fit to tell me of your assignation,' he said. 'It is well.'

'I may go?'

'Indeed you may, in fact you may deem it that I order you to go.'

'Thank you, my lord. I trust, even before this, we shall have better news of the Lady Anne.'

Again the Duke smiled sardonically. 'I doubt it, Piers. The

King will be unapproachable for business for some time, but for the moment we must hope that both ladies will be safe, but find out all you can during your meeting with Alicia at the Golden Cockerel.'

CHAPTER FIFTEEN

As Gloucester had prophesied, it was almost impossible to acquire an audience with the King during the days immediately following his return from Tewkesbury. His Grace was wearied and desired to rest and relax with his closest friends. His councillors were bidden to make decisions without him and not trouble him with wearisome matters of State. His quarrelsome brothers tried his patience to breaking point and peevishly he bade them depart from court and settle their differences amicably between them.

Richard, furiously angry at his brother's treatment of him, stormed into the Royal apartments at Westminster and demanded justice. There he found George, smiling sardonically and refusing to give ground.

'The Lady Anne is promised to me, brother,' Richard grated, his hand flying towards his sword.

'But the Lady Anne does not desire to marry, at present, dear brother,' Clarence replied, suavely, 'would you be ungallant and force the maid into a distasteful match?'

'Distasteful?' the King said, half-bewildered, 'but I thought she was willing.'

'Edward, consider. The poor girl is shocked beyond measure at the death of her betrothed husband. She cannot, in decency, consider marriage at the present.'

'I prefer Anne to live with our mother at Baynards Castle as you promised me, Edward,' Richard said, appealing to the King, 'I want her there, where she will be safe.'

Angry colour flooded Clarence's florid, handsome face. 'Do you dare suggest she is in any form of danger under my roof? By God, I shall forget you are my father's son and . . .'

Edward rose, an angry frown creasing his brow, and stepped between the furious brothers.

'There shall be no brawling here,' he said, in a tone which brooked no argument. Sullenly, Clarence turned away and flung out of the chamber.

'Then keep that crippled fool from meddling in my concerns,' he called, as he departed.

The King thrust a detaining hand across the door as Gloucester sought to follow. 'Steady, Dickon,' he said quietly, 'George is far gone in wine, would you take offence at his drunken brawlings?'

Richard drew a hand across his aching forehead and limped over to the other end of the room. 'One day it will come to bloodshed between us,' he said shakily, 'I'm sorry, Edward, I lost my temper.'

'And well I know it. George would try the patience of an archangel, but for once, I think he speaks truth. Leave the maid alone for a while, with her sister. Later, we will arrange your marriage and the disposal of her half of the Warwick fortune, which forms her dowry. Don't you think it wise? Come now, answer me.'

Faintly smiling, Richard turned and bowed to his brother. Poor Edward, anything for peace at the present moment.

'You promise me you will not let the matter rest here,' he said, 'you and the lawyers will look into it?'

'Have I not promised that Anne Neville shall be yours?' the King said, his tone indulgent. 'Leave the matter with me, Dickon. I have spoken.' And with that, Gloucester had to be content.

On the following Thursday, Piers went to the Golden Cockerel to keep his assignation with Alicia. As usual, he was greeted with great cordiality by the jovial innkeeper and his rosy-cheeked daughter.

As they went through the tap-room, Piers said, 'I am expecting Lady Alicia, so can we have your parlour to ourselves for a while?'

Bess looked at him sharply, and he frowned, a little puzzled by her scrutiny, then, realising the reason, he grinned and flung down his gauntlets on to the polished table. He was still grinning when Jake came in and he tried hard to compose his features at once.

'How went it, lad? Were you wounded?' he enquired gravely.

Piers told him of the two battles. He gave a lively account of his timely rescue by Gloucester.

When Bess came with ale, he asked about Alicia.

'She is not yet here, Master Piers. Rest assured, I will bring her straight here when she arrives.'

Piers frowned. 'She's late,' he said, 'I hope she manages to get away.'

'She will come if she is able,' Jake boomed, as he rose to his feet and lumbered to the door, 'be sure of that, lad.'

'That's what concerns me. I know naught but trouble would keep Alicia from the Golden Cockerel this afternoon.'

'Oooh, Master Piers,' laughed Bess, collecting up the tankards, 'you know what lasses are. Perhaps she mistook the time, or has stopped to look at some frippery or other in the Chepe.'

Piers shook his head in a doubtful gesture but said nothing. That did not sound at all like Alicia. He was sure that nothing frivolous or unimportant would keep her from her appointment with him. He sat on alone in the little parlour, for both Bess and Jake excused themselves in order to get on with the normal routine of the inn. From the tap-room he could hear the sounds of tankards being slapped down upon the small, rough tables. Abruptly he rose, pushed back the chair and walked over to the window. So many times he had stood here and looked down with a never tiring fascination on the noise, and bustle, mud and stench, that was London.

An apprentice, bouncing up and down before the shop, like a dancing bear at the fair, was calling his master's wares in a hoarse voice across the street. Two doors away, the draper's wife, from an upper window, emptied a pail with a slosh into the gutter, narrowly missing an elderly notary, who shouted abuse at her as he hurried by. Piers smiled faintly, then suddenly leaned forward to get a closer look at a slight, girlish figure hurrying down the street. Skirts held high for greater speed, she slipped and slithered a little on the greasy cobblestones. Undoubtedly it was Alicia and in a great hurry. He watched her enter the inn and then turned from the window, as almost immediately he heard the sound of her feet hurrying through the tap-room and up the short flight of stairs that led to the upstairs parlour.

He hastened to open the door for her and agitatedly she sped past him into the room. He could see at once that she was greatly disturbed. Her breath was coming in painful gasps and her face was white and strained.

'Alicia,' he said worriedly, 'dear lady, what ails you?'

She sank on to the wooden chair and dropped her head on to her hands and broke into terrified sobbing.

Thoroughly frightened Piers dashed to the door and shouted for Bess, then returned to her side and dropped to his knees before the chair. 'Dear lady,' he whispered, 'do not weep so. You break my heart. What is it? Surely I can help.' The only answer he got was a tearful shake of her head.

Bess, hurrying into the room, stared in amazement at the weeping girl. 'There, there, my lady,' she crooned, 'tell Bess all about it. What is it?' The sobbing continued for a few moments more, but at last it seemed to have spent itself and the girl sat foward, face hidden, while little anguished quivers shook her slim shoulders. It seemed an age before she looked up and desperately attempted to control her trembling lips. Piers reached out tentatively and took one cold hand. He waited quietly for her to speak.

She swallowed hard, and wiped away the tears from her cheeks with a dainty wisp of cambric. 'I should not have done that. It's the reaction. Here I am among friends and I . . . just let go.'

'Of course, but what is it – the Lady Anne?'

She nodded, then looked away, biting her lip so hard that he saw a thin trickle of blood well up on it. 'Yes, Piers, she's gone.'

'Gone?' he stared at her in astonishment, 'gone where?'

'I don't know, that's just it. I have been looking for her everywhere. She has disappeared.'

There was a horrified silence in the little room. Jake Garnet paused in the doorway as he heard the words. Hearing Alicia come in, he had come up as soon as he could get away from the tap-room, in order to welcome her.

'But no one can disappear into thin air. She must be somewhere,' Piers said desperately. 'When did it happen? When did you last see her?'

'This morning, early. Later, I went out. Dear God, I should never have left her alone . . . ' Alicia once more broke down and buried her face in her hands.

'Now, my lady,' Jake rumbled quietly, 'try to pull yourself together and think. What happened? Did someone come and take her away?'

'No, I tell you, she disappeared. No one knows where she is.'

'But they must. Doesn't Clarence himself know?' Piers demanded.

'He swears he doesn't, that he is as mystified as the rest of us, but in my opinion he has hidden her himself.'

Jake Garnet grunted warningly. He moved carefully to the door and barred it, then nodded meaningly in Piers's direction.

'Tell us what happened when you got back to the house, my lady,' Piers said quietly. 'Take your own time.'

'I must have been out about an hour and a half. I went straight up to her apartment when I got in. She usually stays up there and works at her embroidery frame or reads.'

'And she wasn't there?'

'No,' Alicia shook her dark head emphatically, 'and there was no sign of her anywhere in the house. Lady Isobel and the Countess had seen nothing of her. We waited and waited, but she did not return. We thought there was just a possibility that she had slipped out of the house alone for a walk in the city, but that was doubtful, as the Duke had strictly forbidden it.'

'Did Clarence treat her badly?' Piers asked bluntly. Alicia hesitated.

'No-o,' she said at last, 'but she was not happy there, you understand?'

Piers nodded, stood up and paced the floor. 'Could she have deliberately run away and sought sanctuary?'

'Without me, Piers? Would she really have done that without letting me know where she had gone?'

'You are sure she did not secrete a note anywhere in the room?'

'Quite sure. That is why I was late. I wanted to be sure there really was nothing. I searched everywhere. When Clarence arrived, Isobel told him the news. He seemed flushed, as if he had been drinking. Then he shouted and blustered and raised the whole household to a search, but to no avail.' Alicia pushed back damp tendrils of dark hair, which had escaped from her hennin on to her forehead. 'Jake, will you and Bess leave me, just for a moment, alone with Master Piers?' she said, her voice becoming more steady now, 'and you will say nothing of what you have heard, my friends, I know I can trust you.'

'That you can, my lady,' Jake said heartily, 'now don't take on so. We'll find her. Leave it to Gloucester, *he* will if anyone can. Come, Bess,' with another comforting glance in the stricken girl's direction, he beckoned his daughter from the room.

Alicia watched as the door closed, then looked up at Piers with an enquiring expression. 'Can we do just that, do you think, leave it to Gloucester? Oh Piers, he must find her. I am afraid . . . so afraid for her.'

'But Clarence dare not do her a mischief.'

'Piers, while Anne Neville lives, Clarence has no right to the whole of the Warwick fortune. It will be divided if Anne marries.'

Piers stared at her aghast. 'Then you think . . . '

'I have no right to think anything,' she cut in swiftly, 'but it is to Clarence's benefit that Anne should die.'

He turned away. 'Gloucester must know of this at once,' he muttered.

She called him back from the door. 'Piers, he does love her?' she questioned, softly.

'Yes, Alicia, I believe Gloucester truly loves Anne Neville,' he answered steadily. Her eyes swam with tears and she gave him a slight push.

'Then go to him swiftly. Go with God.'

Once out in the street, Piers mounted and rode to the Westminster Palace. He knew that Gloucester had gone there for the afternoon, seeking an audience with the King. The ante-room was crowded. A steward demanded his name and business and requested him to wait while he sought the Duke. Piers stationed himself close to the door. He was so intent, watching the ladies and gentlemen of the court, that he did not notice the Duke's entry into the room, until he felt a tap on his shoulder.

'You are in search of me, Piers?'

He turned hurriedly. 'Your pardon, my lord, for a moment I had taken my attention from the door. Yes, my business is urgent.'

'Come into the corridor, Piers, we can't talk here.' He limped out of the room and down the corridor until he was well out of eavesdropping distance from the court, then turned a white, strained face to the boy's gaze.

'What is it?'

'The Lady Anne has disappeared from the Duke of Clarence's house, my lord.'

'What?' The word was jerked out in a hoarse, broken voice.

'I have come straight from Alicia. The Lady Anne has gone and left no trace. The whole household is distraught.'

'Could she have escaped into sanctuary?'

'I know not, my lord, but would she have gone without a word to Alicia?'

The Duke slapped his thigh with a nervous hand. 'No, lad,' he grated, 'I think not. I think not.' He moved away about three steps and stood staring into space. 'Order my horse,' he said at last. 'I shall leave for Baynards Castle at once.'

'And the King, my lord?' Piers asked timidly.

Gloucester's lips curved into an openly contemptuous smile.

'While the King is surrounded by this group of chattering monkeys in court dress we shall get no satisfaction here. No lad, if aught is to be done, we must do it. I shall take my men and search every house of ill repute in London. I shall move heaven and earth to find her, and please God, let it be soon.'

CHAPTER SIXTEEN

Gloucester's ardent prayer was destined to remain unanswered. For weeks, he feverishly searched every street and alley way in London without success. The King, when once he heard the disturbing news, ordered his brother every assistance in the search, but all proved unavailing. There was no sign of Anne. Each time his men-at-arms brought the same report, as they rode in, 'No news, My Lord.'

Piers and Guy strode disconsolately about the castle and the London streets. Piers feared to meet Alicia and see the steadily growing dread deepen in her eyes. Guy had no comfort to offer. Both minds were filled with an impending sense of horror neither dared put into words. One thing only puzzled Piers, the attitude of the Duke of Clarence, who seemed as frantic as everyone else about the missing girl. Either he was the most complete dissembler imaginable, or something had him distinctly worried.

It was in this gloomy state of mind, that Piers found himself in Westminster one afternoon some weeks after his fateful meeting with Alicia at the Golden Cockerel. He was to visit Caxton's shop to deliver an order for a Book of Hours for the use of the Duchess of York. Had he not been so perturbed about his failure to assist Alicia, he would have found a keen sense of enjoyment in the visit, for, in spite of his early antipathy for reading, the master printer's shop had a wealth of fascination for Piers. Both the King and the Duke of Gloucester were frequent visitors to the shop, for they had become acquainted with Master Caxton while they had been forced to live in exile abroad. It was at King Edward's invitation that the little printer had set up a press, here in London, the first of its kind in all England.

Today, the shop was crowded, for distinguished patronage had gained the printer added custom. Even so, Piers's livery earned him the deep respect of a young apprentice who hastened behind the shop to acquaint the printer of his presence there. Piers cast but a fleeting glance at the workmen and when Caxton himself came forward and bowed low to him, he gave his order and on receiving a promise that the matter would be dealt with at the earliest possible moment, took his departure. He turned over in his mind the possibility of a visit to the Golden Cockerel. Jake and Bess would be delighted to see him, but he dreaded to face even their questioning eyes and have to repeat the phrase, 'Sorry, no news.' It was while he was considering this that he became aware of the shabbily dressed woman ahead of him. How strangely she walked. Her steps followed a zig-zag course along the cobbles. Could she be drunk? Piers watched her doubtfully. Clearly, she needed assistance. Suddenly her basket, heavily laden with market-produce, fell to the cobblestones with a clatter, spilling vegetables and pats of butter into the roadway. Abruptly, Piers broke into a run. There was no sign of anyone else in the street. The woman was now standing, clutching her breast and her breath came in little painful gasps. He repented of his earlier suspicions concerning her condition. Obviously she was feeling extremely ill.

'Madam,' he said hurriedly, as he drew level with her, 'I see you are unwell. Let me assist you.'

At the sound of his voice, the woman turned and stared at him. Piers had a momentary vision of violet blue eyes and a well-known, delicate, flower-like face, now drawn and pale with suffering, before she swayed towards him and he caught her in his strong arms.

'My Lady Anne,' he whispered and looking down, saw that she had fainted. For a fraction of a second, he stood there, staring at her. It was impossible to marshal his thoughts clearly. He had found her, Alicia's beloved Lady Anne, and somehow he must get her some assistance. Only for a moment did he stand there, then lifting her easily to his shoulder, for so wasted was she that she seemed like a feather weight in his arms, he set off at a run for the Golden Cockerel. Jake would shelter her until he could find Alicia.

He plunged down a less-frequented alley and, seeing no one about, paused before an animal's drinking trough. Gently, he lowered the Lady Anne to her feet, steadied her with one arm and sprinkled a little of the water into her face. She came painfully to consciousness and clutched at his sleeve in an agony of fear.

'Piers – Piers Langham, let me go.'

'My lady,' he said gently, 'you are ill. You need help.'

'Piers, for the love of God, leave me alone. Forget you have seen me. I must be free of the court.'

Even as she spoke, a spasm of pain contorted her lovely face and she bit back a sharp cry. Alarmed, Piers rested her against his shoulder. 'My lady, near here there is an inn kept by some friends of mine. At least come with me and rest there awhile, until you are feeling stronger. You will be quite safe there, I swear it.'

She looked at him steadily for a moment, then nodded. 'You are sure they can be trusted?'

'I would gamble my life on it.'

She straightened herself without speaking and very slowly they continued their journey. Near to the inn, Piers cautioned his companion to wait in the shadows near by, while he went in search of Jake.

He found him in the stables and quickly told him what had happened. The innkeeper's face expressed concern.

'You will shelter her for a while, Jake?' Piers begged.

'Of course, lad, but it seems to me she needs a woman's care. Bring her in the back way, up the stairs and into the parlour. I'll find Bess.'

'God bless you,' Piers whispered fervently and dashed back in search of Anne. She was standing where he had left her. The colour in her cheeks was heightened unnaturally and she was in the throes of a bout of coughing.

'Come, my lady,' he said, taking her arm, 'I have arranged it.' She went with him unresisting and he led her across the road and into the inn.

Bess took charge in the parlour. She took the Lady Anne to rest on a low day-bed and bustled about, preparing food. Piers said quietly, 'Would you like to see Alicia, My lady?'

An eager expression sprang into her eyes, then dimmed as suddenly as it had come. 'I would, Piers, but you must take care. Alicia must not be exposed to any danger.'

He smiled somewhat grimly. 'Never fear, Madam. I have as little desire to embroil Alicia in any peril as you have.'

It was not far to the Duke of Clarence's town house, so Piers did not wait for the innkeeper to saddle a horse for him, but went on foot. On the way, he considered how best to obtain conversation with Alicia. He was dressed in the livery of the Duke of Gloucester, not an attire to bring him into the favour of the Royal Duke, and his talk with Alicia must be in private. The courtyard to the house appeared empty. Piers hesitated for a moment, then quietly unsheathed his dagger and sped softly across the yard and into the stable. There was no one there. One horse moved in its stall, another whinnied in sudden surprise. He drew back into the shadows and waited. In a few moments a young boy hurried into the stable. He stood in the doorway and glanced about him.

'Softly now, my beauty,' he said, 'what ails you?' As if in answer, the animal whinnied again and trampled restlessly about in its stall. The boy advanced farther into the shadow of the stable to find out the cause of the disturbance. 'What is it, Sorrel? There's no one here.'

Piers moved quickly. With his dagger pointing meaningly at the boy's back, he whispered in his ear, 'Don't turn round. Stand still and you are in no danger.' He felt a shiver of fear run through the youngster and smiled a little grimly. 'Do you work here?' he grated.

'Yes, master, I'm an ostler.'

'Know you Mistress Standish?'

'Yes, sir.'

'Is she within?'

'I believe so, sir.'

'Could you get word with her, without arousing undue comment?'

The boy nodded. 'Yes, sir, I think so.'

Piers withdrew his dagger point from the boy's shoulder-blade and turned him round to face him. 'Now listen. If you can persuade Mistress Standish to come here to me, within fifteen minutes, without any other in the household knowing, I will reward you well.' He took out a gold piece and held it out in the palm of his hand. 'Do you understand?'

The boy's eyes widened. He stared at the coin, swallowed, then nodded. His eyes took in Piers's livery and again Piers smiled grimly. 'If you play me false, I shall see that you are punished. I can do that. I see you realise that I am someone to be reckoned with.'

Again the boy nodded, then he looked up at Piers and said quietly, 'You do not wish Mistress Standish harm? If I thought that, I would die sooner than betray her.'

Piers's smile this time was devoid of any grimness. 'Bless you, no lad. I'm a friend of hers.'

'You swear it?'

Piers took out his Christopher medal and held it out towards the boy. 'I swear by this,' he declared simply.

'Then I will do it. What am I to tell her?'

'Tell her Piers Langham must speak with her in haste.'

'You are Piers Langham?'

'Yes.'

The boy gazed at him curiously. Piers gave him the coin, then he hurried out of the stable. Piers stood where he was, as he had no desire to attract the attention of any other groom or retainer in the Duke's service by making the animals still more restless. He bit his lip and frowned. He was in a difficult position. The rift between his master and Clarence had generally widened of late and if Clarence guessed he knew aught of the Lady Anne's whereabouts he would stop at nothing to once more have her in his keeping. How did he know that the young ostler would not play him false? He waited in a fever of impatience, for every second counted, while he stood within the enemy camp, likely at any moment to be discovered, should a servant enter the stable.

As he heard steps approaching the stable door, he gently withdrew his dagger once more from its sheath and drew back farther into the dimness. A shadow crossed the door, then a soft voice whispered, 'Piers, where are you?'

He sheathed his dagger and stepped towards her. 'Did anyone see you come?'

'I don't think so. Abel warned me to be careful. He is a faithful lad.' Her brown eyes opened wide, as she saw his grim visage. 'What is it, Piers – why so secretive?'

He drew her close to him and said softly, 'I've found her.'

Alicia gave a startled gasp then checked it, her hand to her mouth. 'Where?' she breathed.

'At the Golden Cockerel. At least, she is now. I discovered her quite by chance in the street. She is ill. She needs help.'

She turned from him to the door. 'I must go to her. You will take me, Piers?'

'Yes, if you wish it, but Alicia, wait a moment and hear me out. She is in mortal terror, of what I know not. She is terrified of returning to Clarence. I am convinced her life is in danger.'

'I know it. I feared it.'

'We must proceed with caution. Are you sure you want to help me get her to safety?'

'Of course.'

'You realise that once you have done this, you must leave Clarence's household? At the moment you are dependent on him. You were ward to an attainted traitor – where would you go? How will you live?'

'Now is not the time to think of such things. I go where she goes. Take me to her, Piers.'

'Very well. Get your cloak, yes,' he stopped her as she was about to argue, 'you must. A woman without a cloak would attract attention and we want no creature of Clarence to notice us. Besides, who knows how long you will be out? Can you get a spare one for my lady?'

'Yes. Am I to bring anything else?'

'Money and jewels. Any you can lay your hands on easily, nothing else, we haven't time. I shall be twenty yards or so along the street. Be swift now, Alicia.'

'I will. Bless you, Piers.' She touched his hand fleetingly then hurried away. He waited till she was clear of the yard, then recrossed it himself and hurried out of the gate.

When Alicia joined him, about twenty minutes later, she was hooded and cloaked and bore a covered basket on her arm. She smiled up at him as they hurried along.

'Did anyone see you leave?'

'No. Charles Beaumont was in the hall but he did not appear to notice me unduly. I don't think we need worry. Oh Piers – how is she?'

'Not well I'm afraid, but Bess is caring for her. It's her mental state I'm more concerned about.' He related hurriedly how, quite by chance, he had noticed and gone to the Lady Anne's assistance and as he finished, they were before the Golden Cockerel.

'In the back parlour,' he whispered and nodding hurriedly she sped up the stairs before him.

The Lady Anne was sitting up on the day-bed, a little more colour now in her wan cheeks, but her eyes were still unnaturally bright and her breathing somewhat laboured. At the sight of Alicia, she held out her arms with a little sob and the girl stumbled towards her. Laughing and crying a little, as women will, they embraced.

'How is she, Bess?' he enquired worriedly.

'Very delicate, Master Piers,' the girl said, shaking her head. ' 'Tis careful treatment she needs, I'm thinking, if she's to live long. Quiet and rest is what she must have and no excitement.'

Piers stared at her aghast. 'Is it that serious?' he said anxiously.

'It is that. Poor thing. She doesn't look to me as if she has ever been strong and the shock of losing her father like that, to say nothing of what she appears to have suffered, 'as nigh on turned her head. Pity she 'asn't a powerful husband.' Bess clattered away below stairs and Piers walked over to the window, conflicting thoughts awhirl in his head. How on earth were they to get a sick, helpless woman like Anne Neville out of the reach of the powerful Duke of Clarence? He shook his head in bewilderment and sank down on to the window seat.

'Piers.' He looked up as he heard his name called, and Alicia said, 'Come over here, will you?' He rose, and crossing to the bed, smiled down reassuringly at the pale, flower-like face of Warwick's Anne. 'No one followed us here, my lady. You are quite safe.'

'You are kind.' A half-smile curved the pale lips. 'I am feeling better already, thanks to you both, but I cannot be safe while I am here in London. Clarence hates me. He will kill me. You think I am mad, imagining things, but I swear I heard him plotting with one who serves him. They plan to make it appear like an accident. My litter was to be attacked and I killed in the general mêlée. I was a fool ever to trust him. He treats Isobel badly – his own wife. She is half-terrified out of her wits. All he wants is power – power and land. To obtain these, he will betray and kill, destroy everything in his way. I was mad to go with him from Gupshill.'

'My lady, why did you not throw yourself on the protection of the King?' Piers said quietly.

She gave a short, bitter laugh. 'Can I expect mercy from Edward of York, when my own father betrayed him and I was betrothed to Edward, Prince of Wales? At best, he would but return me to the care of Clarence.'

'But . . . ' Alicia hesitated, 'there was Gloucester. Could you not trust him?'

'I thought I could, once.' The girl's voice dropped and became faint and monotonous, as if she were talking in a dream, 'But even he is lost to all honour. He murdered Edward at Tewkesbury . . . and he is too loyal to his brother to help me, now that I am alone and unprotected. I tell you, I can trust no one. I escaped from Clarence's house, taking just a little money. I wandered through the streets of London, terrified of being discovered. At last I went to a cook shop in the Chepe and asked them to give me employment. They seemed sorry for me and took me in, but I have been in mortal terror that they would betray me, for I'm sure they must have suspected my identity.'

'What you must have suffered,' Alicia whispered. 'If only you could have let me know where you were.'

'I dared not try to communicate with you.' Anne coughed weakly and Piers noticed, horrified, that the kerchief she held to her lips bore a faint stain of blood when she removed it.

'I must escape – go abroad. I am not safe here in England.'

'But my lady, how can you?' Alicia whispered. 'You are not well. Where would you go? Who would care for you?'

'I would get employment as a seamstress – anything I must get passage from England.' She looked up appealingly at the two of them. 'You will help me? I have no one I can trust but you.'

Alicia looked helplessly at Piers over Anne's head. Her brown eyes were filled with dread. She spoke dully.

'Very well, if that is what you really wish. I have brought some money with me. We will go together and trust to the mercy of God. Piers shall go and book a passage for us, now, this moment.'

Piers opened his mouth to remonstrate, but she shook her head warningly and her eyes flashed meaningly. Anne turned her violet eyes to him, her face alight with new-born hope.

'You will do that for me, Piers?'

He looked down at her, his eyes troubled. For one moment he hesitated, caught Alicia's eye, then smiled.

'Aye, my lady, anything for you.'

'Then you will go, now, at once?'

'I promise.'

She lifted her tiny white hand and he kissed her fingers, then picked up his cloak and moved to the door. Alicia followed him with the basket.

'Come outside, Piers,' she said quickly, 'and I will give you money.' She drew him out of the room and a little way along the passage.

'Are you mad, Alicia?' he said hastily, 'can you really dream of taking her out of England, two girls alone, without a protector? She would not survive the voyage, I'm telling you.'

'I know it.' Her brown eyes looked gravely up at him. 'Of course she cannot leave England. It would kill her. You must go now to Gloucester and bring him to her, here.'

He stared at her. 'You would have me betray her trust in us?'

'Yes. It is the only way. There is no hope else. You say he loves her?'

'Yes, I know he does, truly, but can we force her to turn to him?'

'He must win her trust. I tell you, it is our only hope.' She looked away from him. 'Do you think I would play her false for aught else?'

Piers stared down at her white face, then he lifted his shoulders philosophically and let them fall. 'My own good sense tells me it is the wisest course – but it goes against the grain to betray a maid who trusts in me.'

'You must, for her sake and mine.'

'Very well.' He started down the stairs when she stopped him. 'Piers,' she whispered, 'take care.'

He smiled. 'Never fear, lady,' he said, 'I will.'

Jake had saddled a horse for him. He mounted and rode hard for Baynards Castle. He found the Duke reading in the quietness of his own apartments. Piers stood in the doorway and spoke, jerkily, his breath coming in hard little gasps.

'My lord . . . Lady Anne Neville is at the Golden Cockerel . . . with Mistress Alicia Standish.'

The Duke stood up, closing the book with a sudden snap. For one moment, his eyes blazed, then he limped forward and placed one hand on the boy's shoulder in an affectionate grip.

'Thank you, Piers,' he said.

Richard took the first horse to hand. Piers flung himself into the saddle once more, as they took the road at a gallop.

The Duke flung a word of command at his captain, who was crossing the yard and Piers knew that, in a few moments, there would be twenty archers armed and ready to protect Anne Neville, to accompany them. At the door of the inn, Piers paused and looked back at his master, earnestly.

'My lord, she begged me not to betray her. She is in mortal terror. Be gentle.'

The Duke nodded impatiently, then mounted the stairs and threw open the door.

Anne Neville was standing, looking out of the window, and she turned with a frightened gesture as she heard the door opened thus abruptly. She stared at the doorway, her eyes suddenly brimming with tears.

'Dickon,' she whispered brokenly. 'Oh, Dickon.'

He moved towards her, then, regardless of the others in the room, gathered her to his breast. 'Anne, my little love,' he murmured, as her bright gold hair covered his shoulder, 'Oh, my darling, at last I have you safe.'

'I was frightened, so frightened,' she whispered, hiding her face against the rich velvet of his doublet.

'I swear you never shall be again,' he said gently, as he drew her tenderly towards the day-bed, to rest.

Piers looked up at Alicia, who nodded imperceptibly.

'It's all right, Piers', she said softly. 'It's all right. She is quite safe – now.'

CHAPTER SEVENTEEN

Piers smiled with genuine pleasure as he prepared to accompany Richard of Gloucester on his first visit to the Lady Anne Neville. It was over a week since they had conveyed her, under armed guard, to a respectable house in the Sanctuary of St Martin's, where she could be safe from any threat of Clarence. Gloucester remained undisturbed by his elder brother's ravings when the truth was out. The King, annoyed by the renewed violence of the quarrel and at the same time relieved to hear of the girl's safety, once and for all put his foot down and agreed to Richard's marriage with Anne.

'And please God, make it soon, Dickon,' he had said testily. 'I'm sick of this whole business. Take the girl into your house and let the lawyers draw up a settlement of your estates. Then perhaps we can have some peace.'

Richard grimaced slightly. It was all very well for Edward to talk like that but he was better built for proposing to a maid. She had run to his arms fast enough that afternoon in the Golden Cockerel, true, but was that only gratitude, the relief of seeing him and not Clarence? He had no way of knowing.

'Piers,' he said, putting down the mirror on the chest before him and swinging round to face his squire, 'come here. I want to talk to you.'

Slightly mystified, the boy came over and stood by Gloucester's chair.

'I received a message from the King this morning. It concerned you.'

'Me, my lord?' Piers's voice expressed astonishment.

'If you will cast your mind back to the somewhat distasteful memory of Tewkesbury, you will no doubt remember that he remarked that when he was once more settled in London that he would be able to more worthily reward you.'

'By, my lord, I desire naught . . .'

'I haven't finished, Piers,' the Duke interrupted coldly. Piers flushed and remained standing, his eyes on the rushes strewing the chamber floor. 'His Grace has at last remembered those promises. On the twenty-first day of this month, he will knight you at Westminster.'

Piers rocked on his feet and stared at the Duke wonderingly. 'You are jesting, sir.'

The Duke's mobile eyebrow rose in sardonic amusement. 'Piers, you will remember I never waste time in such a fashion.'

'But he cannot knight me. I . . . well I . . . am not nobly born. I do not deserve this honour.'

'Piers, do you suggest that my judgement plays me false?'

'My lord, I don't understand.'

'I will explain. I personally requested the King to honour you. Guy Tremaine will win his spurs with several other of your friends at the same time. I wish it. Do you understand?'

'Yes, my lord, but . . . ' Piers's voice trailed off uncertainly. 'Well?'

'Does that mean I must leave your service?'

'No. I should be glad to accept you as one of my household, but you had best be considering your coat of arms for the heralds to be working on. Have you any ideas?'

'No. Such a thought never entered my head.'

'Well, you had better work fast, for you haven't much time.'

Piers murmured a faint assent. His head was swimming with the magnitude of the news he had received. Even now, he could not believe it possible – that he, Piers Langham, was to be a knight.

Gloucester was silent, wrapt in thought on the short ride to Sanctuary. Here in this strange little city all its own, men and women alike lived secure from the laws of men. Once a man, no matter how black his crime, reached this part of London, he was protected by the Church and unless he ventured forth from it could not be arrested and punished. The Sanctuary was full of thieves and murderers. Gentlemen suspected of treason walked among the dirtiest and lowest of pickpockets. Gloucester had placed several of his men within easy reach of Anne's lodging, so as to be sure she would be safe from annoyance. The two were admitted at a little gate by a porter and proceeded from there on foot.

Richard was welcomed at Anne's lodging, and in the hall he divested himself of his cloak and hat. A serving man respectfully led the way upstairs. Alicia opened the door to the two men, curtsying low.

Anne Neville rose to her feet, for she had been sitting near to the fire, an embroidery frame before her. She sank down in a low, graceful curtsy, her delicate face flushed with pleasure.

'My lord, you are welcome,' she said, holding out her hands to her visitor. Richard limped across the room, lifted her white hand and raised it to his lips.

'I am right glad to hear it, madam,' he said.

She smiled. 'Will you not be seated?' and indicated a chair opposite her own.

Gratefully, the Duke seated himself. Piers leaned his back against the door and glanced awkwardly at the pair, then looked back at Alicia.

She was mocking him, he knew. Her eyes were alight with laughter under her dark lashes.

Both ladies seemed to be transformed since he had last seen them. The Lady Anne looked surprisingly well, although she would always appear frail. Her slim figure was clad in a gown of the deepest blue, trimmed with silver. A small circlet of silver held her fashionable veil of the finest gauze, which hid every particle of her lovely golden hair. He turned from his contemplation of her ethereal loveliness to find a changed Alicia by his side. She was small and ever would be, her head hardly reaching to his shoulder, but she held herself with uncommon dignity. She was clothed in red, which only served to contrast her dark beauty. There was little shyness about Alicia Standish. She was laughing at him still, her lips curved with merriment, at his awkward stare.

'I think,' she whispered gaily, 'we are what the French call "de trop".'

' "De trop?" ' he repeated stupidly.

Still smiling, she nodded and pointed to the door. 'In the way.'

'Oh, but the Duke may need me,' Piers stammered.

Alicia gazed back towards Gloucester and grinned wickedly. 'I think not,' she said firmly and led him unprotesting out of the room into the hall below.

For all his service in high places, Piers had never become accustomed to the society of gentlewomen, for his time as an esquire had been spent in camp, on the battlefield or on the march. This elegant, beautiful young lady, who was smiling now at him made him feel just a trifle uncomfortable. On other occasions, when the two had met, there had been so many other matters of importance to fill their minds that Piers had never had time to consider her beauty or her station. Now he had leisure to really look at her, he felt unaccountably tongue-tied.

'Come to the fire, Piers,' she said. 'It is still chilly outside.'

He moved nearer to her and said a little hesitatingly, 'Do you think things will turn out all right?'

She eyed him questioningly. 'Between the Duke and Lady Anne, you mean?'

'Yes.'

A little secretive smile played around the corners of her mouth. 'Oh, I am sure it will.'

'You think she will consent to be his wife?'

'Yes.'

'She will be able to come out of Sanctuary and take her rightful place at court,' Piers said, reflectively.

Alicia held out long slender fingers to the blaze. 'Yes, that will be pleasant.'

'You will enjoy the feasting and the masques and the tournaments?'

She eyed him cocquetishly. 'What woman would not?'

'I suppose so,' he agreed, somewhat grudgingly.

'What *is* wrong with you, Piers?'

He flushed hotly. 'Why, nothing.'

The sound of her laughter filled the hall. 'Oh but there is. Come, what is it?'

'Well,' he agreed reluctantly, 'I suppose they will soon be arranging your marriage.'

'Perhaps,' she said, with a light toss of her head.

'To Beaumont?'

'Oh, I think not.' She took a seat on a carved oak settle before the fire and arranged her wide scarlet skirts to her satisfaction. 'Marriages are a matter of money. The Earl of Warwick, who was my legal guardian, is dead, and the lawyers are arguing who is my rightful guardian at present. Clarence claimed me, but I have since asked the King to either order my estates himself or appoint another to act for him. It is hardly likely that an arrangement will be made between the King and Clarence, for 'tis said they are on bad terms.'

'Do you care for him?'

'Who?'

'Charles Beaumont, of course.'

She stared at him curiously. 'Why should I? I hardly know him.'

'Guy Tremaine says that women are foolish over such things and care only for luxury and titles.'

'It would be better for Guy Tremaine to hold his tongue and not discuss matters he knows naught about,' said Alicia tartly.

'But Alicia, do you *want* to marry?' Piers pressed.

'I want a home and children of my own – someone to love.'

'Love!' Piers said contemptuously, 'from what I hear about it, there is little enough of love in such affairs. Dowries are handed over and marriage alliances made. I wonder you can so lightly think of giving up yourself to some wealthy knight of the King's choosing, for a title or some land.'

'Piers, let us change the subject,' Alicia said, somewhat coldly, her eyes growing steely, 'or we shall quarrel and that right soon. Have you no news for me?'

'Not that I know of – oh yes,' he said, recalling suddenly that he had, 'but I have. The King has promised to dub me knight on the twenty-first day of the month.'

Piers was unprepared for her reaction. With a little cry of joy, she jumped up and threw her arms round his neck, all womanly dignity forgotten in her delight at his news. He felt himself going hot with embarrassment. 'Oh tush, 'tis nothing.'

'Oh but it is, to win your spurs. I have heard the gossips, Piers, talk of how well you fought and your womanish friend Guy, who can fight like a tiger, they say, when all that he loves is at stake.'

'Yes, Guy will be glad to win his spurs. He is relieved that the wars are over. I believe all he wants is freedom and quiet to read in peace.'

'Not by any means a bad desire, Piers,' she said gravely.

'I suppose not.'

'When you are Sir Piers, you will be able to think of marriage.'

'Oh no, not that. I shall never marry.'

'Nonsense,' she said gaily, 'think of the honour and family name you must carry on. What shall you have on your coat of arms?'

'I don't know,' he frowned. 'Gloucester asked me the same

question. I've been puzzling my brains over it.'

'Well, what would you like? The herald will draw out a design for you.'

'I think,' he smiled suddenly, 'yes, I think I will sport a stallion on my shield. Beaumont, I remember, once called me "The Stable Knight". When people attach a nickname to you such as that, 'tis best to accept it, make a jest of it. Aye, Alicia, I shall be "The Stable Knight" with horse and spurs as my device to show my origin in the stables.'

'Who will be your sponsors?'

'I don't know yet. I hope that the Duke will be one, although it is asking a great deal. Yet I know, he personally requested the King to knight me. I wish . . . ' he broke off with a light laugh, 'oh, well, never mind what I wish. Ah, here comes the Duke now.'

The wish that Piers had suppressed hastily was to be fulfilled in a most unexpected circumstance. A week later, he accompanied the Duke on a visit to Westminster Palace. The Duke strode off, leaving Piers to his own devices and, finding no one he knew, he retired to stand dejectedly by the door. He was surprised when summoned into the presence of the King by Lord Hastings, the Lord Chamberlain.

King Edward was as usual seated at his ease on a couch with cushions at his back, and it was easy to see that he was in a rare good humour.

'Come in, Piers. I'm glad Will was able to find you so easily. Sit down, lad, there on that stool.'

Piers bowed, kissed the royal begemmed fingers and sank down near to the couch on the stool which the King had indicated.

'You are wondering why I sent for you,' he said genially.

'Aye, my lord,' Piers replied respectfully.

' 'Tis a matter of little importance, and yet I would have it settled. You will be knighted on the twenty-first of this month. You know that?' The King lifted a hand to check Piers's flow of gratitude. 'You have won the honour fairly enough. You would have been knighted on the field, but that I would not rob you of the delights of the formal ceremony. Some fair maid shall fasten on your spurs for you, but,' he grinned as Piers flushed hotly, ' 'tis of the ceremony I would speak with you. You must have two sponsors.'

'I know, my lord. The Duke of Gloucester says he will stand

for me and so will Sir Francis Lovell.'

The King nodded and lifting a nut from the dish at his side, cracked it between his strong fingers and popped it into his mouth. 'I have promised to confer knighthood upon you. It is your right to expect as much, but if, some other conferred that honour, say, my brother Gloucester for . . .'

Piers almost upset his stool in the movement of delight. 'Your Grace, if that were only possible.'

'Um,' smiled the King again, 'he is not very complimentary is he, Will, to prefer a mere Duke to Edward of England?'

'Your Grace, I would not offend you. 'Tis just that I love His Grace of Gloucester so deeply.'

The King laughed heartily. 'Think naught of it, lad. Leave the arranging to me. You must have another sponsor, of course, but we'll see to that, eh, Will?'

Hastings smiled in answer and the King dismissed Piers with a wave of his jewelled hand.

He walked unseeingly along corridors, his mind already envisaging the pageantry shortly to take place. He was quite close to the Queen's apartments, when he heard a voice he recognised. It came from the length of corridor ahead, at present hidden from his sight by an angle of the wall.

'Let me pass, Master Beaumont, at once, please.' The tone was icy, yet Piers quickened his step as he detected a faint note of anxiety in Alicia's voice.

Turning the angle of the corridor, he saw her attempting to enter a room, but her way was barred by a handsome, fair-haired youth who lounged across the doorway.

'Not so fast, Mistress Standish,' he drawled, 'at least let me see more closely the face that is soon to be mine.'

'I fear you are mistaken, sir,' she retorted, 'please let me pass.'

He smiled but remained where he was, so that she was forced to give ground a little. 'Have you forgotten a certain marriage contract drawn up, to give me your money?' Here he made her a mocking little bow, 'Though pray forgive me for mentioning it and for your part of the bargain, you will one day be my countess.'

'I have not forgotten it, sir. That contract was never made legally binding and even now the matter is being decided by the King's lawyers. Whatever happens, know this – I would sooner die than wed with you.'

'So your mistress said, I remember once, about her marriage

with Crookback, but I fear that she is finally about to give him half of the Warwick fortune. What choice has she? He needs the money and I hear has the charm to make his wooing pleasant enough when it suits him.'

'You unspeakable cur,' Alicia whispered, her voice hoarse with anger, 'Gloucester married my mistress for love, a word you don't know the meaning of. Now let me pass before I am forced to cry for assistance.'

'That will not be necessary, Mistress Standish,' Piers interposed quietly. 'I am here and with your leave will attend to this matter.' He moved towards the two, his face grim and set.

'Ah, our gallant Stable Knight to the rescue. Bravo, I understand that you really are to bear the title, Knight. My congratulations to Gloucester if he can really succeed in making a gentleman of you.'

'Stand away from the door, sir,' Piers said, his voice dangerously quiet.

Beaumont's lips curved in a sneer. 'Do you think I will take orders from a stable hand?' he said jeeringly.

In spite of his determination not to lose his temper, Piers's fingers strayed instinctively to his dagger.

'Piers no – be careful,' Alicia whispered warningly. 'There must be no trouble here.'

Piers turned and looked at her meaningly and shook his head gently once, then turned to Beaumont. 'I believe, sir,' he said, 'you heard the lady express a desire to go into that room. Pray stand away from the door.'

Beaumont moved indolently, but his blue eyes were now as steely as Piers's own.

'Did you hear me?' Piers said, his voice rising slightly.

'I object to brawling with rabble, but I warn you, Langham, stay out of my affairs.'

The two stood staring at one another, breathing heavily. Alicia seized her opportunity and wrenched open the door abruptly.

'One day,' Piers said, speaking calmly and distinctly, 'I shall make you pay for your insults.'

'Can a peasant be insulted?'

'By God,' Piers hissed. 'That's enough.' He drew his dagger and the two closed with each other. Beaumont moved with lithe grace. His own weapon was already in his hand and he parried Piers's thrust with a mocking jeer.

'No, Piers, no,' Alicia called desperately. 'Both of you, stop it. Do you hear me?'

Neither took the least notice of her and she moved backwards into the room behind, her eyes following the flickering blades, her heart full of icy dread.

'You've interfered in my affairs long enough,' Beaumont snapped. 'My intended bride is my own concern.'

'You foul cur, you endangered the Lady Anne by your deliberate lie and for that . . .' Piers grated.

'Drop those daggers at once, both of you,' a curt voice snapped out from the doorway behind. Both men stood still. Alarmed by Alica's anguished cry, people had flocked to the scene from the adjoining room. Piers looked up to see Lord Rivers, the Queen's brother, bearing down on them.

'Sheathe those weapons at once. Do you not know it is treason to draw a weapon in the Palace? Men have lost their hands for less. This brawling is to cease.'

Charles Beaumont laughed softly and with a graceful gesture sheathed his dagger.

'Your pardon, My Lord, just a stupid quarrel over . . . ' he shrugged expressively, 'well, no matter, nothing of importance. Tempers ran high and it came to this.'

Rivers nodded shortly and turned to Piers. 'This quarrel is not to be renewed,' he said evenly. Piers nodded. His weapon had fallen to the floor and he stopped and picked it up.

'This affair is over,' the Earl said, with a wave of his hand. The little group began to disperse. Beaumont whispered a word to the Earl, tossed his fair head to Piers in a mocking gesture and strode off. The talking and laughter died down at last and Piers found himself alone with Alicia.

'Thank you, thank you, Piers,' she whispered.

'He dared to annoy you. By God, I'll make him pay.'

'No.' She placed a soft hand on his arm. 'Please, be careful, he is dangerous. Watch out for yourself, for my sake.'

He looked up to see the Lady Anne staring at him intently from the open doorway behind them.

'Piers,' she said quietly, 'I would like to walk in the garden. Will you accompany me?'

'Why, my lady, of course.'

'Alicia, I shall need a wrap. It is chilly. Will you get it for me and come down to the yew walk?'

'Yes, my lady.' Alicia gave Pier a half-curious glance and went out off through the door.

Anne Neville and Piers went out into the sunshine of the Queen's privy garden.

'It is so peaceful here, such a retreat after all we have gone through. It makes me dream of Middleham, my home,' she said musingly. 'You have never been to Middleham, Piers?'

'No, my lady.'

'Richard has promised to take me home, when we are married.' She moved on, stooping now and then to examine a plant or spray of blossom. At the end of the walk was a small wooden seat under an oak tree. She seated herself and looked up into his face.

'What lie was it that Charles Beaumont told me, Piers?' she questioned softly.

He had expected this and looked away hastily. 'Why, my lady, I . . . I don't know . . . '

'Please, Piers, what was it? I have a right to know.'

He stubbed his toe awkwardly against a stone to cover his embarrassment. 'His Grace of Gloucester said I was not to speak of it, but since you must know – he lied when he said the Duke murdered Edward of Lancaster. The Prince was killed in fair fight, truly my lady.'

She was silent, staring in front of her and he went on, 'No one knows who killed the Prince, but I swear it was in the heat of the battle.'

'You saw it?'

'No,' he hesitated and she prompted him gently.

'Well, Piers?'

'I saw him – afterwards.' He stopped and moved round to the back of the seat. 'It is not good to think about, Madam. He had been trampled by the horses and men in the retreat.'

'This, then, is possibly why Richard did not wish me to know?'

'He did not wish you to be unduly distressed, my lady.'

She held out her hand in a simple gesture of friendship. 'Thank you, Piers. Thank you so much. You do not know how much this knowledge has helped me. Now, here comes Alicia with my wrap. Thank you, dear.' Alicia slipped the velvet cloak over her shoulders, and Anne smiled. 'Leave me now, both of you. I'd like to be alone.'

She sat and watched them move off together and smiled a warm, happy smile. Then she looked up as a familiar sound broke her rosy daydream. Richard was approaching, leaning on his cane. She rose and moved towards him, her face radiant and her heart singing with happiness.

CHAPTER EIGHTEEN

Piers sat still on his truckle bed and listened to the noise outside in the corridor. It was past the hour when most people were abed, but tonight no one would retire very early. He had just changed into his new finery when the Duke of Gloucester entered and announced that he would accompany him to the chapel.

As they entered the courtyard before the chapel, a slim, cloaked figure withdrew herself from the shadows and came towards them. 'May God guard you and give you strength, Piers.' His lips trembled as he saw Alicia smiling up at him, the light from the torches shining on her face, making it ethereally beautiful. Piers bent to kiss her hand.

'You will pray for me?'

'Of course. I would like you to have this with you tonight.' She held out a golden cross which he had glimpsed several times round her throat and he took it and looped its chain over his fingers.

'Thank you,' he said, for he knew nothing else he dare say. She smiled, curtsied to the Duke and hurried back to her apartments.

He stared after her for some moments, watching her slim figure outlined against the lighted doorway, and then disappear into the Palace. How could he tell Alicia Standish that he loved her and would until he died? Marriage with a lady of so high a rank was inconceivable. When Alicia was given in marriage it would be to someone with rank and breeding, never a Stable Knight.

He had laughed at himself for entertaining so forlorn a hope and yet it seemed that his heart would break with the pain of it. He loved her laughing eyes and lips, her luxuriant dark hair, her dainty feet and hands and that coquettish jerk of her head and the laugh which always rang out at his clumsy awkwardness.

Gloucester had withdrawn himself a little when Alicia came to speak to him. Now he came forward. 'Ready?' he asked quietly.

'Yes, your Grace.'

'Then we will go in.'

Piers caught his breath at the beauty of the little private chapel, where he knelt holding his sword up before him. He felt, rather than saw, the Duke kneel at his side for some minutes, then he rose and touched Piers's shoulder in a hard, comforting grip, then limped up the aisle and away from him. Piers heard the click of the great door as he went out, leaving the four squires alone with God.

Turning his head a little, Piers saw Guy before the Shrine of Our Lady, his lips moving in prayer. He knew that the other two knelt too, in the stiff, straight attitude which they must maintain until the morning.

Gradually the light of dawn stole into the chapel through the stained-glass windows and great stronger until the four smiled at one another and shivered slightly in the first chilly air of morning. Their long vigil was almost over. At last, Piers heard the click of the latch and the priest walked up the centre aisle towards them to hear their confessions.

Later, the sun streamed forth in its full glory, touching with its light the glitter and gold in the courtyard and making it seem slightly unreal. Stands had been erected on three sides of the court for the ladies and gentlemen. The King himself was clothed in scarlet trimmed with ermine. His golden hair hung to his shoulders, while the uncut jewels in the magnificent collar at his throat glittered and shone as they caught the sunlight.

In contrast to his elder brother, Gloucester seemed slight, almost effeminate. Only those who had seen him in action at Tewkesbury and Barnet could have guessed at the strength lying latent in the slender form. He was smiling now, colour tingeing his usually pale cheeks. The harsh scowl and worried frown which had aged the youthful face had recently faded in the first flush of his new-found happiness.

Beside the King lounged the Queen, lovely as ever in cloth of gold, by her side the Lady Anne in a gown of pink overlaid with silver. Shyly, Piers lifted his gaze to meet Alicia's laughing eyes. Today, she seemed farther beyond his reach than ever. Her gown of blue brocade with its wide long sleeves falling to the ground, the sapphires she wore at her throat and unfamiliar grotesque headdress like a huge butterfly poised for flight, made her seem like some grand lady, only her dark eyes, alive with mischief, twinkled and flashed at him in the old, teasing manner.

In a heart-warming speech, the King thanked the four squires for their services to the Yorkist cause and one by one, they stepped forward to receive their rewards.

Piers touched his dry lips nervously with his tongue. Now at last, it was his turn. Sir Francis Lovell and Sir Richard Ratcliffe moved to his side. He murmured his thanks as they led him forward to stand before the King.

King Edward, tall and splendid, stood with his jewelled sword in his hand and he smiled deliberately at Piers. Out of the corner of his eye, he saw Gloucester rise and come forward, ready to sponsor his squire as custom demanded. The King's voice cut across his intention.

'You, Sir Francis, and you, Sir Richard, do you as ancient custom demands, sponsor this squire, Piers Langham, and request his knighthood at our hands?'

They bowed their heads and solemnly answered the King. 'We do, your Grace.'

Piers saw an angry flush dye Gloucester's cheeks and he turned abruptly away from the royal dais. The King smiled teasingly and held out his heavy jewelled blade towards his brother. 'Your privilege, brother,' he said quietly.

There was a little pause and Piers waited in an agony of doubt. Gloucester turned back, looked up at the King wonderingly, then down at Piers.

'Is this what you want?'

'Yes, your Grace.'

The Duke stepped forward, bowed to the King and took the jewelled sword from his hand. 'Kneel,' he said crisply to his squire.

Piers dropped to his knees and felt the flat of the sword touch first his right, then his left, then finally his right shoulder once again, and the Duke's voice say in a clear, ringing tone, 'In the name of God and St Michael and St George, I dub thee Knight. Be brave, adventurous and loyal.'

He stood up and was embraced by Gloucester, who said smiling, 'My felicitations, Sir Piers Langham.'

The royal ladies flocked to the four new-made knights. Piers found himself surrounded by the chattering throng. He knew that the Lady Anne helped to fasten on his golden spurs but it was Alicia who bent to buckle round him his sword blessed and consecrated and brought from the chapel, where he had lain it on the altar and dedicated it to God.

He ate little during the banquet which followed but watched fascinated as the food was served; the boar's head raised high by the servants, roasted peacock, duck, pheasant, larks' tongues, birds stuffed and garnished and flavoured with all kinds of strange and varied spices and herbs. He had watched banquets such as this many times, but today this one was in his honour and he sat among the gentlemen of the court, above the great salt cellar, the symbol of his newly acquired rank.

When at last the feast was over, the King took his departure from the hall. He stopped before Piers. 'Come to my apartments, Sir Piers. My brother and I would speak with you,' then, linking arms with Gloucester, continued his journey out of the room. Piers bowed low and followed.

Edward sank down lazily in his great chair and gestured to both of them to seat themselves. 'My brother tells me you wish to continue in his household, Sir Piers.'

'That is so, sire.'

'Good.' He nodded content and indicated a document which lay on a table near him. 'I have made over to you the Manor of Brampton in Kent. It is confiscate to the Crown and will bring you a reasonable income,' then he grinned as Piers stared at him, not comprehending his meaning. 'I understand it has a good bailiff. It need not cause you undue concern. He will handle your affairs and, meanwhile, you can continue to serve my brother.'

Piers dropped on one knee and kissed the jewelled fingers which held out the document for him to take.

'Your Grace, how can I show my gratitude?'

The genial smile faded and the King looked down at him gravely, then placed his hands on Piers's shoulders.

'Continue to serve my house loyally,' he said, 'for there are few who serve the great and are truly sincere. Now go, Lad, for I would confer with my brother.'

Piers hurried through the Palace and knocked on the door of Guy's apartments. Luckily he found his friend alone and told him of his good fortune. Guy's face flushed with pleasure.

'Now, no one can dispute your right to gentility.'

'It can never be forgotten that I came from the stables.'

Guy put out his hand and abruptly turned his friend round to face him. 'Never let it be forgotten. You won your spurs by loyalty to the King's cause and gallantry in the field. That is more to be proud of than an honour bestowed by right of birth or lands gained by an advantageous marriage.'

Piers smiled warmly in answer. 'You are a good friend, Guy. I won my spurs by sheer luck, by the friendship of Alicia and the favour of Gloucester.'

'And you have done valiant service for both of them. By the way, how lovely the lady has become.'

'Yes,' Piers said and once more turned away. Guy gave a low sibilant whistle. 'Aha, sits the wind then in that quarter, my friend?'

Piers turned his shoulder back hurriedly. 'Don't be an arrant fool, Guy. How could it?'

Guy lifted his shoulders in one of his amused enigmatic gestures and lightly let them fall. He changed the subject, but his eyes continued to smile.

In the apartments laid aside for the use of the King's younger brother, Richard of Gloucester sat at his desk. He tapped the quill pen lightly against his teeth and frowned at the document under his hand. What was he to do for the best? It was all very well for his beloved Anne to say that . . . His line of thought was interrupted by a light tap on the door and he called a hasty, 'Come in.' A page ushered in Mistress Alicia Standish, who curtsied low, her head demurely lowered.

'You sent for me, your Grace?'

'Yes. Come in and sit down, Alicia.' He indicated a chair and rose until she was seated opposite to him. Looking down at the lovely face before him, he was even more bewildered. Womanlike, she arranged her skirts to her satisfaction, clasped her hands demurely in her lap and lowered her mischievous dark eyes. He scrutinised her bent head, for a moment in silence, then abruptly cleared his throat.

'Alicia,' he said at last, 'you know that the King has decided to make you a ward of the crown. He has asked me to take you to ward. I trust that meets your approval?'

She lifted her expressive dark eyes and they were wide and innocent. 'Indeed, your Grace, I accept gratefully whatever the King decides in the matter of my welfare.'

Gloucester's lips twitched in spite of himself. The girl's

duplicity was amazing. He had a shrewd suspicion that she herself had arranged this matter to her own satisfaction, but he said nothing. God help the poor fool who marries this maid, he thought, with an inner grin, for she'll twist the soul from his body with her bewitching eyes and airs of injured innocence.

'It is left to me to arrange your marriage. You will understand that I prefer you to wed with one who pleases me?'

'Oh yes, your Grace.'

'I take it you are not in love with young Beaumont?'

'No, my lord.'

'Good. In that case, you will be prepared to marry someone in my household, one whom I favour?'

She looked up at him, a hint of mischief in her eyes. 'I would please Your Grace in everything.'

He held her gaze with his own for some moments, then he grinned broadly. They understood one another perfectly, though neither said one word.

'It is well,' he said at length, briskly, 'and now, my lady, you may leave the matter in my hands. Never fear, I'll arrange a suitable match.'

She rose and curtsied. He watched her elegant, proud young figure, until she was out of the room. He once more smiled and then picked up his quill and resumed work on the papers before him.

Piers was still laughingly conversing with Guy when he was summoned to the Duke's apartments. He found the Duke preparing to change.

'Piers, I want to talk to you and while I do it you can assist me.' Gloucester peered into the mirror at the reflection of the young man behind him. 'I want you to do me a service. It will require some spirit of self-sacrifice.'

'Indeed, sir?' Piers said, his eyebrows raised slightly as he laid a selection of jewels on the chest for the Duke to choose what he would wear for the evening.

'The King has given into my charge one of the royal wards. I have to arrange a suitable marriage for the girl. Would you be prepared to take her to wife? She has some considerable fortune.'

Piers stiffened, then recovering himself, bowed slightly. 'I am prepared to do what you wish, sir, but what if the maid is not willing? Am I to force a match? I am not of noble birth.'

The Duke frowned arrogantly. 'Be not willing? Nonsense.

144

She will do whatever I wish her to do. Her wishes need not enter into this discussion. Are *you* willing? That is the only thing that need concern us.'

'Yes, your Grace, if this match pleases you.'

'It does please me.' The Duke turned slightly and scrutinised Piers's face. 'There is no one else? Your affections are not engaged elsewhere?'

Piers flushed. 'No, sir, I . . . I did not deem myself of sufficient importance to look at any maid with a desire to marriage.

'Of course you must marry and raise up fine sons to serve our house loyally.' He smiled faintly as he moved to the door. 'I will send my ward to you. Await her here and make known to her my wishes. The marriage contract can be drawn up within the next few days.'

Piers bowed and answered formally, 'I will, your Grace.'

Piers heard him move away down the corridor. His lips tightened involuntarily and his grey eyes showed the intensity of his suffering. He moved to the window and gazed bleakly out over the ordered garden with its neatly clipped yew hedges and beds of sweet-scented herbs. Of course he was a fool to think this way. Alicia was highly born and not for him. By this marriage, he would please Gloucester. Since marriage with Alicia could not even be considered, if marry he must, why then what did it matter to whom? He turned automatically as the door opened.

'My Lord of Gloucester said that you wished to speak with me,' he heard a sweetly familiar voice say from the doorway. Alicia, unbelievably beautiful, came towards him across the room.

'Why no, you must have been mistaken – at least – he said . . . ' He broke off and stared at her hard. For one moment her eyes laughed at him, then were quickly veiled by her long silken lashes. Piers looked down at her in silence. He passed a hand over his forehead as his thoughts began to take shape.

'Gloucester told you to come here to me?' he said at last.

'Why, yes. Haven't I just said so?'

'Then *you* are his royal ward?'

'Yes, by order of the King.'

'I see.' Piers stood still, continuing to regard her gravely. She frowned and tapped her foot impatiently. 'Well?'

Piers stared at her wonderingly.

'What do you want? Why did you send for me?'

'I . . . ' Piers drew a sudden gasping breath. 'I . . . ' he stumbled awkwardly, 'well, Alicia, His Grace of Gloucester said . . . er . . . well he said . . . '

'Well, Piers,' she cut in impatiently, 'What *did* His Grace of Gloucester say?'

Piers moistened his lips nervously and brought it out with a rush. 'He commanded us to wed, Alicia.'

'Oh.' Her reply was noncommittal.

'Have you nothing to say?' he queried earnestly.

'What should I say, Sir Piers? It is the Duke of Gloucester's command.'

Piers came a little nearer. 'Do you wish it?' he insisted, in a voice that was a trifle harsh. He was staring at her so intently now that she flushed and dropped her head.

'Why I . . . '

'Alicia, will you wed with me of your own free will?'

She was silent for a few moments and he stared worriedly down at her bent head. Suddenly her shoulders began to shake uncontrollably.

'Alicia,' he said quickly, 'what ails you?'

She lifted a face flushed with laughter she could no longer conceal.

'If you would have it in plain words, fool, why else do you think I manoeuvred it so that the King would give me into Gloucester's care – for who else would Gloucester choose but . . . '

Piers took her fingers and imprisoned them within his own. 'Who else would he choose but me?' he said quietly.

Laughingly, teasingly, she lifted her face to his.

'Who else, but you?' she said.

CHAPTER NINETEEN

'Job Stanton says that the King has offered an arrow of pure gold for the champion at the butts. The grandstand will be draped in cloth of gold and . . . '

Piers turned from the window to listen, smiling, to his young page's excited chatter. The boy was furiously polishing his helm. 'Cease your chattering and hurry with that armour. I'm going now to attend his Grace.' He walked to the door and said over his shoulder, 'You will want me to look my best this afternoon, I am sure, Geoffrey.'

The boy's excitement was understandable. Today the King was to stage a gigantic tournament at Smithfield, in honour of his victory at Tewkesbury. For a week now, workmen had been busily engaged in preparing the ground and erecting stands to seat half the nobility of the Kingdom. Piers was looking forward to the event as keenly as his page, for he wanted an opportunity to show his prowess. Always proficient with sword and lance, Piers knew that here he would, for the first time, show to the world his new surcoat emblazoned with the black stallion on its silver ground. With the help of God, he hoped not to disgrace it.

That afternoon Piers stood in the doorway of the silken pavilion, where he had assisted the Duke of Gloucester to arm, and surveyed the scene. The great grassy oblong had been tended and rolled till it resembled a rich green carpet. At both ends, fenced off from the lists, were two immense pavilions, gaily bedecked with ribbons and bunting. On one long side of the arena was the grandstand, draped in cloth of gold, and bearing the King's personal device of the Sun in Splendour. Along the opposite side, the packed masses of town and country people pushed and jockeyed for position. They had come from miles around to see the colourful pageantry.

Already, the King and Queen had taken their places on the

stand, while the heralds had proclaimed the name and rank of all taking part in the jousts. Beside the Queen sat the Lady Anne and with her Alicia. Slouched on the King's left sat his brother Clarence. He alone of the royal three had refused to take part in the day's pageantry. His face was blotched and bloated from heavy drinking and his weak, lax mouth wore a perpetual sneer. His wife, Isobel Neville, had made a valiant effort to hide her tears from the curious, impersonal stares of the crowd. As Piers watched, he saw her eyes dart from her husband to the King and then from him to Gloucester who had just emerged from the tent, and her expression was heavy with foreboding. The King repaired to the pavilion where he donned armour and helm to ride with his brother into the lists.

With the other knights, Piers rode behind the King and the Duke down the length of the lists towards the royal stand. He was mounted on a superb coal-black charger, a present from the Tremaines, and for the first time held steadily before him his shield with its sable stallion rampant on a ground of argent. His newly acquired motto was inscribed in English in the new style and read simply, 'THROUGH SERVICE TO THE HEIGHTS'.

Alicia smiled as Piers tipped his lance in salute and dropped down to him a gauzy blue scarf. This, her favour, Piers raised to his lips and carried back with him to his pavilion, where his page tied it securely to his helm.

The King and Gloucester took the field against the King's brother-in-law, Earl Rivers and Lord Hastings. The King rode well, as ever. His opponent, Hastings, fell to the ground as the King's blunted lance struck him squarely as he thundered past. Hastings ruefully accepted defeat and appeared unhurt as he made his way towards the opposite pavilion.

Gloucester's surcoat bore his personal device of the White Boar. A little murmur went up as he rode into the lists to face his opponent, Earl Rivers, as all knew there was some feeling of rivalry between them. The young Prince, badly handicapped by his deformity, had won the hearts of the townsfolk by his valour on the field at Barnet and Tewkesbury. Silver trumpets blared out the challenge and the two combatants settled their lances and rode with a thunder of hoofs and clouds of dust towards each other. Heavy blows sounded on the shields and, as the two parted, Piers saw that neither was unhorsed. A full-throated roar of approbation went up from the ground, while the King grinned delightedly. Once more the two carefully balanced their lances and rode determinedly towards the other. Gloucester swerved skilfully to miss Rivers's lance and turning, struck squarely at the other's shield. To do so, he pulled his mount about with such speed, that it reared, forelegs high in the air, and only by superb horsemanship was he able to keep his seat. The Earl fell from his horse with a thunderous jarring sound and the bout was over.

Piers hurried forward to assist the Duke to divest himself of his breastplate and helm. He was flushed with victory and smilingly acknowledged the plaudits of the crowd as he limped to his seat by his brother's side.

When the silver trumpets sounded again, Piers thrilled to the sound. It was a challenge to prove his mettle. With the three other young knights the King had favoured, he rode into the lists. Alicia was sitting tensed in her seat and he fancied that her hands were clasped tightly in her lap.

Piers found delight in the clash of weapons, the keenness of the wind against his cheek and good horseflesh between his knees. Lance splintered against lance, horses squealed, shields thundered together and men fell heavily into the dust. After half an hour Piers and Guy, flushed and dishevelled were yet in the saddle and rode their horses towards each other rejoicing in their victory. It was done. He had proved his new coat of arms. Heads respectfully lowered, the two received the gracious words of congratulation from the King.

He was halfway to the pavilion when he saw a familiar figure ride his stately white stallion towards the royal stand. There was no mistaking that fair head and erect, disdainful carriage. It was Charles Beaumont. The crowd was hushed abruptly as his voice rang out over the packed arena.

'Sire, I claim a privilege.'

'What is it, young sir?' The King's voice had a brittle coldness in its tone, courteous though the words were.

'I would challenge one of your knights to combat.'

The King shrugged, looked back at the little group of gentlemen behind him, who looked equally puzzled, then he turned back to the challenger.

'The right is yours. Choose your opponent.'

Beaumont bowed low in the saddle and skilfully turned his mount. Piers had by this time reached the flap of the pavilion and dismounted. He smiled a little grimly as he saw Beaumont's mount approach the door of the pavilion. So be it, he thought. In such a way must I prove my right to My Lady.

Charles Beaumont halted his steed and stared coldly down at Piers. He was elegantly armoured and appeared fresh and in fine fettle for the coming bout. Piers, on the other hand, was fatigued from his recent exertions. The crowd was very quiet. It seemed as if it sensed the hatred between these two and waited, breathless, for the outcome.

Slowly Beaumont drew the heavy iron gauntlet from his hand and threw it down on to the ground at Piers's feet. Piers gazed down at it, then up again at the challenger's face. He bent and retrieved it, then stood for a moment, balancing it in his hand.

'Yours, sir, I believe,' he said pleasantly. 'I am ready to meet you at once.'

Beaumont took the gauntlet and, again turning his mount, rode towards the array of armorial devices which flanked the side of the pavilion. Fastened to the iron rail were seven shields, among them, a replica of Piers's own with its black stallion on the silver ground.

Charles Beaumont struck the shield heavily with the sharp end of his lance. A sudden gasp went up from the crowd. Piers did not take his eyes from the proud mask of the face looking towards him. 'So be it,' he said in a level tone.

Across the lists came an urgent command from a voice that brooked no disobedience. 'Gentlemen, ride before me at once.'

'What is this, sir?' the King demanded frigidly of Beaumont. 'This joust is a friendly demonstration of skill, not an excuse to settle private quarrels. If you desire to show your mastery over Langham, here, surely such a purpose can be achieved without loss of life. Come gentlemen, what is this?'

'I claim the right of challenge, sire.' Beaumont's tone was almost insolent. 'It is for Langham to accept or reject it.'

'I accept the challenge, sire,' Piers said, steadily.

The Duke of Gloucester rose. 'Sire, I request that you forbid it.'

'Peace, Dickon,' the King said quietly, 'I think it is for these two to decide. Come, sir,' he said, once more addressing Beaumont, 'what is it that lies between you?'

'An insult, sire – and the hand of a lady.' Beaumont bowed mockingly towards Alicia, whose face had gone ashen. 'That of the Lady Alicia Standish, who was to have been my wife.'

150

'This is ridiculous,' Gloucester interposed, 'the girl is my legal ward and formally betrothed to Sir Piers of her own free will.'

Again the King indicated by a commanding gesture that he required instant silence. 'Sir Charles,' he said coldly, 'you dishonour your knighthood if you force this encounter. Take back your challenge and agree to meet in friendly joust, otherwise, I warn you, you will incur my gravest displeasure.'

'For that I am deeply sorry, sire.' Again the mocking tone was evident in Beaumont's voice, 'but I will not withdraw my challenge. I fight to the finish, or not at all.'

'You will refuse to accept Piers. It will be no dishonour,' Gloucester grated and the King waited for his answer.

'Sire,' he said at last, 'it is true that there is bad blood between us. I did not desire that this should be the fashion in which we should settle it, but I fear it must be so. I will fight Sir Charles until one or both of us is dead.'

'No . . . no Piers, no,' Alicia gave a choking cry and Piers saw an icy gleam light momentarily Beaumont's eyes.

'It must be so, my lady,' he said quietly.

The King sank heavily back in his seat. 'Very well, gentlemen. Piers, choose your weapons. It is your right.'

'Thank you, sire, If agreeable to Sir Charles, I choose lance, broadsword and dagger.'

'Agreed.'

'Then, sirs, to your pavilions and let us have this bloodthirsty business over as soon as possible.'

The two opponents bowed to the King and to each other. Piers smiled in what he hoped was a reassuring manner in the direction of Alicia's stricken little countenance. He saw Anne Neville draw her to her into a consoling embrace, then he turned his back on Beaumont and rode towards his own pavilion.

Conflicting thoughts teemed through his brain as he prepared for combat. Several times they had matched wits and skill. Now he needed mastery of both to leave the lists alive. He knew that he could not live with himself if he failed to meet the challenge. He became aware of some little stir and noticed that the tournament marshal was checking the armour and weapons at Charles Beaumont's end of the lists.

'Here is your lance, sir,' Geoffrey's face was pale and strained. 'All our prayers go with you.'

He watched as the marshal checked his armour and weapons for flaws and then the pear-shaped foil was withdrawn from the lance, another grim reminder that this encounter must end by the loss of a life.

The trumpets sounded. Piers seized his lance and steadied it in his hands. The wind cooled his over-heated brow. Now that the moment had come, he felt icy calm. He saw nothing of the gorgeous splendour in the royal stand, nothing of the crowd eagerly pushing against the rail which kept it clear of the lists, nothing even of Alicia. He saw only an enemy on a white horse – someone he must do his utmost to kill in the next few moments. His eyes sought the King. There was a sudden flash. His Grace had lowered his hand holding the ornamental silver mace. It was the signal to commence combat.

He touched spurs to his mount and thundered across the grass. He saw the sun flash upon armour, heard lance thud upon shield, then the two were clear again and he was still in the saddle. He wheeled his mount and saw Beaumont, still firm and upright, once more balance his lance. Again he spurred against the other and as his opponent loomed up before him leaned over in an effort to strike. Beaumont parried the blow with his shield. Piers's lance splintered harmlessly against it, but he himself was able to avoid Beaumont's thrust and ride clear. He was now at a disadvantage, for a lance had a much longer reach, while he was forced to come in close for his broadsword to be of use to him.

Again the two horses thundered across the grass. Beaumont lunged and, to avoid the blow, Piers pulled his mount sharply aside. Even so, the weapon pierced his armour, then splintered against his upraised shield. Again they were equal, but Piers felt slight discomfort from the scratch. A sudden roar went up from the crowd. A lucky thrust of Beaumont's had cut across the forelegs of Piers's mount. It reared and he was thrown heavily to the ground. For one frightening moment, it appeared that he was in danger of being trampled by the hoofs of Beaumont's infuriated stallion. He rolled clear, then rising, jumped at the other's bridle rein. He was jerked into the air but he gritted his teeth and pulled with all his might. Infuriated at such unexpected treatment, the white horse whinnied shrilly. Beaumont fought to keep his seat, then he too was thrown to the ground. A yell greeted this move, and those in the royal box sprang excitedly to their feet.

By the laws of combat, neither man could now remount. Piers retrieved his sword and waited, chest heaving slightly, as the other drew his. The crowd made no sound. It waited, tense with excitement for the end of the affair. The King sank back in his chair. He had made a move to stop the combat when Piers was thrown, but was now, once more, content to await the issue.

Piers felt hot anger blaze through him, as he saw Beaumont's mocking countenance close to his own, as they cautiously circled and backed, each parrying the blows of the other. Charles was fresh and less heavy than the country lad and he was easily keeping him at a distance. Piers was fast tiring. The weight of his armour was becoming unbearable and the wound in his arm, slight as it was, was troubling him. He rashly determined to make an end. His blazing anger was clouding his judgement. He lunged, overbalanced and felt sudden agonising pain tear through him as the other's blade found its mark in his shoulder. He slipped to the ground, his weapon falling useless from his fingers. Beaumont stood back, smiling slightly and then came on for the kill. Piers desperately sought to draw his dagger with his left hand. Stupidly, clumsily, he sought to parry the blow . . . then suddenly, he felt the blade touch flesh, felt blood well up to the hilt and in a daze, he beheld Charles Beaumont slip slowly down to his knees, blood staining the grass where Piers's dagger had pierced between breastplate and gorget. The crowd roared, then just as suddenly was still. He climbed unsteadily to his feet and stared down at his antagonist. He took a step forward, swayed, then, lifting his sword with his left hand, for his right arm hung paralysed at his side, he touched Charles's throat with the point of the blade. Beaumont was badly wounded and in great pain, but he smiled a little twisted smile.

'Make an end, Stable Knight,' he whispered, huskily.

'Yield you to me, Sir Charles?' Piers said quietly.

'Aye, the victory is yours.' For once there was no teasing smile on Beaumont's lips. Piers lowered the blade and stood up. The combat was over; Alicia was his. Dimly, he heard the approbation of the crowd, as he moved wearily towards the royal box. He slipped to his knees before the King. 'Will Your Grace pardon me, if in aught I have given you displeasure?' he said.

'Never mind that. Are you hurt, lad?' Gloucester demanded as he came towards him.

'No, Sir. 'Tis but a flesh wound.'

'Sir Charles?' the King rasped meaningly.

'I know not, sire. Pray send a surgeon to him.'

'You should have killed him while you had the chance.' Piers stared up, surprised, at the coldness of Gloucester's tone.

'I could not,' he said quietly.

Squires and pages dashed to the fallen knight and lifting him on to an improvised stretcher, conveyed him to his pavilion. Piers was swaying with dizziness and an ominous red stain was seeping through his armour on to his fine surcoat. Guy Tremaine slipped a firm arm round his shoulder and followed by Alicia, led him to his own pavilion. Gloucester excused himself to the Lady Anne and was about to follow, when the King, speaking in angry tones, checked him. He paused to listen.

'If that fool lives,' he grated to Clarence, 'he is to leave the court and never return. I will not receive him. See that he obeys me.'

Clarence rose, hot anger mottling his bloated face. 'You think to slight me, brother,' he raged. 'Cross me and you will regret it.'

The King drew back, pale with fury that matched his brother's. 'You dare to threaten me,' he whispered. 'By God – do that again and you are like to lose your head.'

'George, take care,' the little Countess's anxious voice broke in on the two and she placed a restraining hand on Clarence's arm. He flung it off impatiently. 'I'll go, before I say more, Edward,' he snarled, 'but heed what I say. Don't cross me.'

Gloucester found Alicia busily tearing up strips of material to make a pad for the wound in Piers's shoulder. He pushed aside the little group and asked curtly, 'How goes it, Piers?'

'Well, sir.' Piers grinned up at him. ' 'Tis naught but a flesh wound. I'll live.'

Alicia nodded to the page, who was kneeling on one knee before his master with a bowl of water. 'You can remove that now, Geoffrey,' she said quietly. 'Rest, Piers, or you will start off the bleeding again.'

'Has the surgeon been?' the Duke asked.

'I sent him over to the other tent. Sir Charles has greater

need of him than I,' Piers replied quickly. 'Tell me, Sir, have I angered the King?'

'Nay, 'tis not you who has angered him,' Gloucester said wearily.

Piers looked up anxiously and the Duke moved impatiently away. 'Don't worry, lad. Just another outburst from Clarence. Let this news go no farther. If you are sure you are all right, I'll go attend the King. Mistress Alicia, will you go to the Lady Anne?'

'Of course, your Grace.'

The Duke paused in the doorway and looked back at Piers. 'Mind what your lady says, Piers. You need rest.'

The group round Piers moved away and he looked smilingly up at Alicia. 'Naught stands between us now, dear lady,' he said. 'You need have no more fears.'

'Piers, I was so frightened. I thought you would be killed before my eyes.'

He turned away. 'I know not what happened, Alicia,' he said huskily. 'I thought my death very near, when suddenly —my dagger found his breast. I felt blood well up on the blade . . . God, I have not killed him. What happened, did he slip?'

'Piers, you are not to think of it. I did not see it clearly. Mayhap, he slipped, as you say, on the grass. It may have been slippery with blood. Think no more of it. You are not to blame if he does die. All knew he meant to kill you.'

His page re-entered the pavilion. 'Sir – Sir Charles Beaumont's squire is outside. He requests that you speak with him. I have told him that you must rest, but he insists.'

'Has Sir Charles asked for me?'

'I believe so, Sir . . . but . . . '

Piers stood up and moved to the entrance. 'I must go, Alicia. You understand that?'

'Very well – but – take care.'

He stooped and kissed her hand and then moved back to the tent-flap and walked across the lists. The crowd had dispersed and already the ground was wearing a forlorn, forsaken look. The great stand was empty and silent. Only the chatter of squires and serving men came from the two great pavilions, where departures were being arranged for those who had taken part in the day's jousts. The cool wind seemed to clear his head and at last he stood outside the entrance to the

155

opposite pavilion. He stooped and entered, almost knocking over a little harassed-looking man who was preparing to depart. His sober houpelande of blue, and studious air, proclaimed his a physician.

'How is he, Master Surgeon?'

The little man paused and looked back at the stretcher where the knight lay. 'I believe he will live, sir.' Another inch to the right . . . ' he shrugged meaningly, 'but there – he must rest. He has lost a great deal of blood, but with care he will be ruffling it again in a month or two. If you are going to him, sir, I pray you not to overtire him.'

'I will not. Thank you,' Piers said gravely, and the little surgeon hurried out murmuring that he wished to make arrangements for Sir Charles to be carried away.

At Piers's approach, Sir Charles's squire left the pavilion, leaving the two alone. Piers looked down at his recent antagonist, whose face was grey with fatigue and pain.

'It was good of you to come, Piers.'

'Are you in pain?'

'Nay, I'm well enough. I wanted to talk to you . . . ' His voice trailed off weakly and Piers said quickly, 'do not tire yourself.'

'Hear me out. First I ask your forgiveness.'

'Willingly granted.'

A wan smile touched the bloodless lips. 'Thank you. My second point is harder to explain, but I will try. I have always jealously guarded my pride of family and boasted of the blood I inherited. I doubted the wisdom of raising yeoman stock to the rank of nobility. Now I know that Gloucester is right. What matter it from where a man springs, if his heart is noble? I feel that this is the beginning of a new thought in England. Men will become famous for wisdom and daring and it will be to such men that the leadership of our race will be given.' He looked away, and continued, 'In fair fight you might have killed me, yet you played a nobler hand and spared my life. Would I had your friendship, Piers Langham.'

Piers was silent a moment, then he said, 'I do not know if what you say be true. Perhaps England will come to rely on her doctors and merchants, as well as her lords and barons. Aye, even her farmers and labourers too; that is far to look into the future, but I am willing to be your friend if you wish it.'

'You will take my hand in friendship?'

'Aye, that I will.'

Beaumont pushed himself up on the stretcher and the two grasped hands, then he fell back on to the improvised pillow. 'I must leave court. I am in disgrace, but one day I pray I may serve you and yours. Now leave me, Piers Langham.'

Piers looked down at him once more, then he stood up and walked away. Outside the pavilion, it occurred to him that in there he had won a greater victory.

THE SYLVIA SCARLETT TRILOGY

by Compton Mackenzie

D. H. Lawrence considered the Sylvia Scarlett saga to be Sir Compton Mackenzie's masterpiece. Covering the same colourful period and including many of the same characters as the classic SINISTER STREET, this story breaks brave new ground in its exploration of a heroine acclaimed as 'one of the few really great women in fiction'.

Sylvia is a beautiful girl with a bitingly sharp tongue. She is married at the tender age of nineteen to the dashing Philip Iredale, and their three-month whirlwind of passion drives their relationship to cataclysmic destruction in SYLVIA SCARLETT. Shattered by a brutal divorce, she throws herself into a hedonistic life in Europe, which prepares her for the second great passion in her life – SYLVIA AND ARTHUR. Finally, in SYLVIA AND MICHAEL, she fights down despair only to be confronted by the horror of the First World War, and her last and greatest love.

'In the great tradition of English picaresque novels – in many ways it is a twentieth century *Moll Flanders*.'
—*Antony Sampson*

SYLVIA SCARLETT   30p
SYLVIA AND ARTHUR   30p
SYLVIA AND MICHAEL   35p

NEW ENGLISH LIBRARY

NEL BESTSELLERS

War

W002 686	DEATH OF A REGIMENT	John Foley	30p
W002 484	THE FLEET THAT HAD TO DIE	Richard Hough	25p
W002 805	HUNTING OF FORCE Z	Richard Hough	30p
W002 494	P.Q. 17—CONVOY TO HELL	Lund Ludlam	25p
W002 423	STROKE FROM THE SKY—THE BATTLE OF BRITAIN STORY	Alexandra McKee	30p
W002 471	THE STEEL COCOON	Bentz Plagemann	25p
W002 831	NIGHT	Francis Pollini	40p

Western

Walt Slade—Bestsellers

W002 634	THE SKY RIDERS	Bradford Scott	20p
W002 648	OUTLAW ROUNDUP	Bradford Scott	20p
W002 649	RED ROAD OF VENGEANCE	Bradford Scott	20p
W002 669	BOOM TOWN	Bradford Scott	20p
W002 687	THE RIVER RAIDERS	Bradford Scott	20p

General

W002 420	THE SECOND SEX	Simone De Beauvoir	42½p
W002 234	SEX MANNERS FOR MEN	Robert Chartham	25p
W002 531	SEX MANNERS FOR ADVANCED LOVERS	Robert Chartham	25p
W002 766	SEX MANNERS FOR THE YOUNG GENERATION	Robert Chartham	25p
W002 835	SEX AND THE OVER FORTIES	Robert Chartham	30p
T007 006	THE CHARTHAM LETTERS	Robert Chartham	30p
P002 367	AN ABZ OF LOVE	Inge and Sten Hegeler	60p
W002 369	A HAPPIER SEX LIFE (Illustrated)	Dr. Sha Kokken	60p
W002 136	WOMEN	John Philip Lundin	25p
W002 333	MISTRESSES	John Philip Lundin	25p
T007 022	THE NEW FEMALE SEXUALITY	Manfred F. De Martino	50p
W002 859	SMOKEWATCHERS HOW TO QUIT BOOK	Smokewatchers Group	25p
W002 584	SEX MANNERS FOR SINGLE GIRLS	Dr. G. Valensin	25p
W002 592	THE FRENCH ART OF SEX MANNERS	Dr. G. Valensin	25p

Mad

S003 702	A MAD LOOK AT OLD MOVIES	25p
S003 523	BOILING MAD	25p
S003 496	THE MAD ADVENTURES OF CAPTAIN KLUTZ	25p
S003 719	THE QUESTIONABLE MAD	25p
S003 714	FLIGHTING MAD	25p
S003 613	HOWLING MAD	25p
S003 477	INDIGESTIBLE MAD	25p
S004 163	THE MAD BOOK OF MAGIC	25p
S004 304	MAD ABOUT MAD	25p

— — — — — — — — — — — — — — — — — —

NEL P.O. BOX 11 FALMOUTH CORNWALL

Please send cheque or postal order. Allow 5p per book to cover postage and packing (Overseas 6p per book).

Name ....

Address ....

....

Title ....
(JULY)